Sam stepped into the open and said, "Easy does it."

They were taken completely by surprise. It was Tim, the youngest, who lost his head. He yelled and jerked up his weapon, loosing a wild shot.

Sam fired. The bullet took Tim in the head and knocked him back against the mountainside, gurgling, bleeding.

As the echo of the shot died Sam said, "Didn't want to do that. Frank, better behave. Put down the guns."

Frank Coleman looked at his dead brother. His voice was choked with grief and rage. "Put 'em down, boys. Put 'em down. This here's Cemetery Jones."

CEMETERY JONES

William R. Cox

FAWCETT GOLD MEDAL • NEW YORK

A Fawcett Gold Medal Book
Published by Ballantine Books
Copyright © 1985 by William R. Cox

Library of Congress Catalog Card Number: 85-90925

ISBN 0-449-12810-5

Manufactured in the United States of America

First Edition: October 1985

It was a high place. Samuel Hornblow Jones sat on the step of the cabin in a lane of afternoon sunlight. A wild burro wandered by, sniffed the thin air, wrinkled its nose, and skittered down a meager trail through heavy brush into a deep ravine.

Sam could see them coming. They were about a mile below the mine. The narrow, difficult road meandered so that they now and then vanished, reappeared. They wore town clothing, the trio, but they rode well, western-fashion, pacing the horses against the climb. Sam's mind ran backward even as he planned ahead.

He had been in the Black Hills for months, too long. He had not discovered the claim; he was not a prospector. He had won the Long John Mine in a poker game. He had, in fact, almost neglected to properly file it under his own name. An assayer friend had advised him to pursue the venture. It had been necessary to learn many things, to invest capital. When Sam had finally struck the vein he'd known at once that he must sell. He had no heart for continuing, to build a safe road up the mountain, to find financial backing for a mill, tying himself to a life for which he had no stomach. He was a veteran of the frontier, he had gone up the trail, an orphan, at age fourteen. For more than twenty years he had tried all that was offered in the towns and on the prairies.

He was not a cattleman, not a lawman, not a professional gambler, yet he had been all three. He had been a lawman, but he had never been a thief. He had seen towns settled, watched them grow, noted the changes as civilization touched the land. He had known the Indian and watched what had happened to him and what he had attempted in self-defense. Time had come in upon him and now he wondered if he needed roots, a home, he who had scorned domesticity.

The three men rounded a sharp turn and he was able to identify them. Jabez Wall was in the lead, clad in black as always. Harrison Deal, the lawyer, sharp-faced, thin, came next. Behind them labored Harp Grogan the ex-prizefighter, now bodyguard, a hulking figure bursting from his striped pants and checkered coat. The sale had been notarized; it was only necessary to hand over the cash as Sam had demanded.

He had wanted cash because he hated paperwork and because he did not trust Jabez Wall. He wanted to get out of the mountain and down to the town. He watched a black bird circle overhead seeking offal on which to feed, a bad sign.

His mind flashed to the woman in town, Renee Hart, who played piano in a way he did not quite understand but which moved him in a strange fashion. He would see her soon and continue the good talk, the good times. She was a handsome lady from the East, somewhat mysterious. She had looked upon him with favor, disappointing several local swains.

Sunrise was a busy town what with the mining and the cattle and the commerce of the high plain. Renee played in the most respectable and profitable saloon, the El Sol. There was only one other female working in the place, Sally McLaine, a young, pert creature, defiant, seeming not to recognize the dangerous future that threatened all of her kind. Sam enjoyed the El Sol far more than he enjoyed the Black Hills.

Now he would be rich, comparatively speaking. He could

indulge himself. He had notions, some old-fashioned, he supposed, some a bit ahead of the times. He was at a cross-roads; he had no definite plans except to enjoy himself.

The three riders came around the last bend in the road. Sam was more than ready; his saddlebags were packed, including the revolvers, and his bedroll was in place on the dun horse. He wore clean, worn work clothing, a loose vest, a red kerchief, and his new boots and Stetson. He arose from the step and went forward.

Jabez Wall climbed stiffly down from the hired hack. "Hell of a road. Goin' to take a heap o' money to get ore down from here. You drove a hard bargain, Sam."

"Yup." Wall was reputed to be a millionaire, yet he was always whining, weeping, carping. Actually, little was known about him and less admired.

Harp Grogan carried a black satchel. Harrison Deal seemed nervous, his breathing shallow in the high altitude.

Wall said testily, "All right, give him the money. Too damn much money, by gum."

Sam accepted the bag, took it to the cabin steps, removed green bills and a poke of gold. He counted it.

Harrison Deal said, "You're a suspicious man, Jones."

"Tried to beat me down, didn't you?" Sam finished the count and went to his horse, storing the money in a saddle-bag. They watched him closely and within him there stirred a small warning. He touched the stock of his rifle in its scabbard.

Harp Grogan spoke, his voice hoarse from the punches that had struck his throat. "Heard you got a monicker. Seems like they call you Cemetery Jones."

"Not to my face." Sam was wary.

"Seems like you put away a lotta people. In cemeteries." Now there was a distinct challenge.

"You say." Sam leaned against the withers of the patient dun.

Jabez Wall interposed, whining. "Now, none of that. The deal's made; let the man go on his way."

"Just wonderin'," said Grogan. "Killers, country's full of 'em. Backshooters, mostly."

Harrison Deal said hastily, "Nothing personal, Jones. We'll look around the claim. You'd better go on, since you're ready."

Sam swung aboard the dun, looked down at them. They were sweating, yet the air was cool. Only Grogan met his direct gaze. "It's all yours." He rode down the trail. He could feel their eyes boring into his back. He came to the place where the stray burro had disappeared. It was an old track that he had discovered months ago when the Apaches were rumored to be in the hills. He reined abruptly onto it.

He thought he heard them shout at each other as he rode from their view. He could not have attempted this trail on another horse; he had to give the mountain-bred, well-trained dun its head. Sam sat loose in the saddle, going down slowly through the pines and the heavy underbrush that clung to the rocks. The dun snorted, seeking tentatively for footing. They were off the main road, but there were places, Sam knew, where an ambush might be laid. He could be wrong, but on the other hand it would be easy to kill him and the horse and fling them deep into the ravine, where the bodies might not be discovered for months. It had been done before and the blame laid upon Indians.

There were rumors about Jabez Wall. He had come up from nowhere and grasped for power with the aid of the slick lawyer, Deal. He had haggled over the price of the mine, thirty-five thousand dollars, yet he had not objected to carrying the small fortune up to the mountaintop. There was something about the man that inspired distrust. There had been something about the aura of the three men as well that had disturbed Sam's sensory system.

The old trail slanted toward the main road. There would be a place where he could be seen, a cul-de-sac. Sam took the rifle from its scabbard. The dun stood well, reins trailing. The path was thorny, but Sam had dwelt with Apaches. He slicked his way along with silent skill.

He caught a glimpse of sun on shining metal. He slowed, dismounted, crawling on his belly. He sighted them in the spot where he had anticipated they might be. He moved closer. He recognized them without surprise. Their pictures were in every marshal's office. They were the Coleman brothers, all four of them: Frank, the elder and leader, Jake, Jesse, and Tim. They were wanted from California to Missouri. They were fugitives on every count under the law. They were train robbers and bank robbers and holdup men and murderers. They had last been seen in Texas; now they were in New Mexico.

Sam stepped into the open and said, "Easy does it."

They were taken completely by surprise. It was Tim, the youngest, who lost his head. He yelled and jerked up his weapon, loosing a wild shot.

Sam fired. The bullet took Tim in the head and knocked him back against the mountainside, gurgling, bleeding.

As the echo of the shot died Sam said, "Didn't want to do that. Frank, better behave. Put down the guns."

Frank Coleman looked at his dead brother. His voice was choked with grief and rage. "Put 'em down, boys. Put 'em down. This here's Cemetery Jones."

They obeyed. Their horses were huddled against the side of the mountain. They bit their lips, ordinary-looking men in clothing too fancy for hard work. They had come through a myriad of gun battles without losing a member of the family. They were in shock.

Sam whistled for his horse. The amiable animal came through the brush. He mounted without taking an eye from the Colemans. He said, "Walk."

"Walk?" They were bug-eyed.

"Like I say."

Frank stammered, "And . . . leave . . . leave Tim here?"

"Your partners up on the mountain'll find him."

Frank gulped. "Podners? What podners?"

"Them that told you I'd be carryin' cash."

"You're loco, Jones. We were restin', layin' low."

"Stick to that. It's safe," Sam told them.

Jesse Coleman said, "I'll be damned if I'll walk. You can drag me afore I'll walk."

"You want it that way, you can have it that way."

Frank said gloomily, "Believe him. He'll do it." He began to walk unsteadily down the road. The others followed, throwing glances back at their dead brother, hanging their heads in disbelieving sorrow. They were stunned in more ways than one, Sam thought, riding behind them. It must have seemed a simple task to waylay one man and dispose of him. And in return, part of the loot and safe conduct out of the countryside—or a continuing partnership therein.

Now he believed what had been whispered about Jabez Wall. Sam had, in his fashion, reserved judgment pending the completion of the deal for the mine. Now he was certain that he had been set up for the kill. It was a matter he would consider at his leisure. He was not a forgiving man.

He well knew that the outlaws shambling ahead of him had weapons concealed about their bodies. He also knew they would not attempt to turn on him while he kept his rifle at hand. They were brave enough, but they were also experienced.

Sam did not relish his reputation. Tim Coleman would not have died if he had kept his head. He shook himself, knowing he must maintain extreme caution, knowing that if sudden darkness or a mountain storm overtook them, there would be problems. Still, he could not refrain from thinking back to the time when he had shot down a crazed, pistol-wielding cowboy in Dodge City. That had been the start. The dead man's friends had made a concerted attack. From a position in the doorway of the Long Branch Saloon he had picked them off. Bat Masterson had been the youngest sheriff in the West in those days. In his whimsical fashion Bat had coined the name "Cemetery Jones."

Bat had befriended him, taught him the many angles of gunplay. Bat's friend Luke Short had taught him useful matters about cards, about how to cheat the cheaters while remaining himself above suspicion.

They had come at him then, the would-be gunslingers, the ones with imagined heroics to uphold. He had the quick hands, he could not run; he faced them and they went down. He never drew first, he avoided argument, he became cryptic in his effort to avoid trouble. He lived by an ethic born of the frontier: be quiet, be sure, and be brave.

The three men ahead of him had a hard go of it on the stony path to Sunrise. Sam had no sympathy for them. They were men without pity, cruel men, sons of crime. If they had hired out to Jabez Wall, all the worse for them. There were men and women and children who had suffered from their depredations. And in this matter, if he was correct, they had sold their lives. An old song came to him and he hummed, "A man can shoot another man . . . and still be on the level . . . But woe and shame will come to him . . . Who sells out to the devil . . ."

Music was natural to him. It accounted for his first acquaintance with Renee Hart when he had not quite understood the magic of her piano but had warmed to it deep in his soul.

Jesse Coleman tripped and fell. His brothers picked him up, brushed him off. Sam Jones wondered what it would be like to have brothers. He had no kith nor kin, nor had he known any since the death of his parents; not cousins nor aunts nor uncles. There was, however, more than that missing from his life. He stirred uneasily in his saddle as finally they came around the bend that led to the last steep slope and thence to the wide, dusty, flat road to Sunrise.

He put aside all cogitation and warily watched for backup guns. If this was a plot of Jabez Wall's fabrication, there could be assurance that the Colemans never would get back to town with the loot, that more reliable people would fake an attempt to put them under arrest even while they appropriated the cash. Possibly Wall had other henchmen who could be trusted further than one could trust the Colemans.

Nothing interposed. They entered the main street without incident. The sun was lowering, bathing the town in colors reflected from the hills. People walked to and fro, wagons rolled, children and dogs romped.

Then movement stopped, all eyes upon the cavalcade, on the sore-footed Colemans, on Sam Jones. The outlaws were easily recognized from the flyers offering a reward for their arrest. There were oohs and ahs and shrill cries from the boys and loud barking from the dogs. The Colemans held their heads high, sneering, swaggering on aching ankles.

The office of Marshal Dick Land was at the far end of the street. Behind it was the jail, iron-stiffened adobe walls, strong timbered roof. Sam tied up and motioned his prisoners indoors, waving negligently at the following crowd.

Land dropped his copy of the *Sunrise Enterprise* and dropped his feet from the desk. He was an aging, rawboned man with a flowing iron-gray mustache. "What in tarnation you got here, Sam?"

"Kind of a crowd," said Sam. "Better button 'em up."

"I God, the Colemans. But where's Tim?" Land asked.

"They'll be bringin' him in."

Frank Coleman said, "And you'll pay for him, Jones, goddamn your soul to hell."

"Yup," said Sam. "Better let 'em soak their feet, Dick. There'll be people askin' questions."

"You walked 'em down the mountain?"

"Safer that way," Sam said.

"They jumped you on the road?"

"Tried to."

"But in all tarnation, why you?"

"Got my own notions about that. I'll write it all down for your reports."

"You better had. Donkey!" Land called.

Donkey Donovan was very young, very large. He came sleepily from the cells and stared in astonishment, fumbling for his keys. "The Colemans? I be galled."

"Most of 'em," said the marshal. "Put 'em away careful-like, Donkey. Search 'em down to the skin while I hold on 'em." He took a big Colt .45 from a drawer. "They come loaded for bear, these people."

Sam sat down behind the desk. He found an official form, dipped a steel pen in ink, and began to write. He put it all down without alluding to his suspicions of Jabez Wall. He signed it and shoved it back.

The lawmen returned with their arms full of assorted knives, derringers, ankle guns, brass knuckles. Donovan took a shotgun from a case and returned to the cells.

Land said, "Damn if you ain't the one, Sam. Trouble walks in your footprints."

"Been here almost a year without any." Sam shrugged. "Got to see Banker Solomon. Toted too much money. Dumb."

"I'll be sendin' out telegrams and such. This here is hot news. The governor put up a thousand dollars t'other day when he heard the Colemans might be around. The newspapers, even those back east, they're gettin' so they got their noses in everything goes on. Must say this here's the biggest grab been made made in a hell of a time. The Colemans, shoot, hell! Next thing to the James Boys and the Youngers."

"Best you put out word no lynchin'. People get riled easy these days," Sam cautioned.

"Don't expect there's much Judge Lynch left around here. Town's calmin' down a heap. Lots of money, plenty jobs. The old days is jest about gone," the marshal said.

"You got the Colemans in there."

"And the Pitman bunch is still runnin' and there's thieves in high places and Apaches in the mountains. And there's me and you, mostly you." The aging lawman saluted and Sam departed.

He unlimbered his saddlebags and walked across the street. People called out, asked questions. He waved them off. The bank was closed. He walked through the alley to the back door and knocked in code. Abraham Solomon peered through an aperture, then admitted him.

Sam said, "Had to see you, Sol."

"It was in my mind that you would."

They went into an office that contained a desk, a table, two chairs, and a huge iron safe. Solomon sat at the table, which served him for various purposes, including a bed for napping during the hot noondays. He was more than a banker; he was part and parcel of the town of Sunrise, an honest man with the weight of his fellows on his bent shoulders. He was bald, with sideburns and a neatly trimmed beard. His eyes were shrewd and piercing.

"You got to learn, Sam. Cash dealings with Jabez Wall, that is not safe business."

"Just a notion. The Colemans proved me wrong." Sam told the story.

"Ah. Yes. And how did the Colemans know about the money?"

"Jabez Wall, I expect."

"Which you cannot prove and I cannot prove."

"He's movin' into Sunrise. Right?"

"True or not true, I do not like my feeling about him."

"Yup. Me neither," Sam said.

Abraham Solomon ran a finger around the edge of his celluloid collar, then made a steeple of his long, veined hands.

"I am going on sixty years of age. When I came here with my Becky there was no need of a bank. Becky, rest her soul, had hard days. Then we had help. From back east. And the town grew and became my town. Jabez Wall we do not need."

"If I'd of known I wouldn't have sold to him."

"How could you know? Now it is too late to do anything but wait and watch."

"If that's enough."

"True. I own this bank. He owns or controls ranches, bits of railroads, this and that. He buys politicians. Cash? He may be short there. Still, the town needs help," Solomon said.

"It's a nice town."

"Strong help. From men like you, Sam."

"Not me."

"You are going to leave here the money?" Solomon nodded at the saddlebags.

"You know a better place?"

"Many. Frisco, Denver. Big cities. Safer."

Sam said, "Could be I wouldn't make it to some other place."

"Ah!"

"Dick Land is a good man."

"Like me, he grows old." Solomon's fingers separated, went back together again. "You like Sunrise."

"As good as any town."

"There is the lady."

Sam said, "Now, Sol."

"I see no difference between a lady playing classical piano in the El Sol and women raising children in a sod house."

"Never mind Renee. You're askin' me to stick around?"

"The circuit judge won't be here until next month. The Colemans, you think Dick can hold them that long?" Solomon asked.

"Sure. Unless they get outside help."

"That's not probable?"

Sam sighed. "Put the money in your safe, Sol. It stays, and if it's here, I'd better be here."

"On the other hand, if we lose the town you could lose the money."

"So? Maybe I owe somethin' to Sunrise. I struck it rich here."

"Nobody owes anything to a place, Sam. To people he owes, and to himself."

Sam nodded. They shook hands, holding tight for a moment, understanding each other.

"I'll be at the hotel," Sam said.

"God go with you."

Sam walked across the street to the dun horse. He was, he realized, weary. When strain was upon him he was not aware of it, but when it was over, the reaction set in. Dick Land peered out a window at him, his face creased with worry. Sam waved at him and walked the horse to the livery stable. He carried his belongings into the Miner's Roost Hotel and a Mexican boy leaped, smiling, to his aid. He went into the bar and drank four ounces of whiskey. He was sweating. He had no notion of escaping into a bottle, though; it was not his style.

He obtained his key and went upstairs. The boy had a tub in the room and was pouring hot water. He handed over a dollar and took off his clothes. Then he remembered to lock the door.

He immersed himself in the tub with a bar of soap and thought about the killing of Tim Coleman. It had been absolutely imperative to stop the man from shooting. But he was not now and never would be certain that it had been necessary to kill. Sam had faced this dilemma before. Living as he had set up within him certain reflexes. Instinct had told him to fire a fatal shot.

His trouble was that where other men notched their gun butts, he wore the notch on his soul. That is, he added to himself, if he had a soul, if anyone had a soul. On such subjects he was unsure. He knew that there should be a reason for being on earth and that he had not discovered it.

If there was a pattern to his life, then the sale of the mine, his demand for cash, and the ambush were all part of a plan. Perhaps there was a purpose behind it all; maybe he was fated to remain in Sunrise as Sol had requested. He had no answers, only unanswered questions.

He dried himself and lay on the bed and fell suddenly into deep slumber. When he awakened it was dark and there was someone tapping on the door. He called out and quickly donned clean clothes. As always, his heart beat faster when he opened the door and saw her.

She wore a full, deep blue cloak with red lining. Beneath it was a long dress designed far from Sunrise. She was tall and her shoulders were squared and her head was held high. Her dark hair was drawn back from delicate ears into a bun at the nape of her shapely neck. Her great, round onyx eyes shone upon him. Her hands, long and slender, reached out to him.

He said, "Renee. I was asleep."

"I thought you might be." She came into the room, closing the door behind her, scorning convention. "News gets around like wildfire in this town."

"I'm okay."

"Yes. It takes a very short time for you to recover. Still, a man dead, bandits corralled." She sat on the bed, divesting herself of the cloak, smiling. Her feet were small, her ankles shapely. She had velvet skin; the sign of her age was only in the tiny lines at the corners of her eyes. "It's nearly time for supper."

He sat beside her, their bodies touching, aware of each other. "They did try to wipe me out, Renee."

"Which has been tried rather too often." Her voice was well placed, not quite western, cultivated. She was from the East, he knew, and there was very little else he knew of her past. When she played the piano men came from miles around and were enthralled. She was not notorious, she had no other love than Sam, but she was becoming famous in the territory. She seemed content, yet there was always a feeling that she might vanish overnight into thin air.

"What will you do now?" she asked.

"What should I do?" He had never asked anyone that question.

"Oh, you'll stay in Sunrise. The western man."

"Cemetery Jones." They had been through this before.

"The name you earned."

"And never wanted."

"So. This time the victim was a criminal who, had he been brought to trial, would have hanged," she said softly.

"No matter."

"I understand, my dear. However, since you brought in his brothers there will be further complications."

"Probably," he agreed.

"A possible feud?"

"Maybe so."

She slipped her arm around him. "Please, Sam. Relax."

"Abe Solomon wants me to stay. I put a heap of store in Sol." They were close; he wanted to stay close to her.

"Sam, we need each other." She had never stated it before. It had, he realized, been taken for granted.

"You give, Renee. You give me a lot."

"Everyone needs at times. Even loners." She sighed. "You don't know anything about me, what I've been and done. You very well might never know."

"In the West we don't ask, remember?"

"That is why I am here. So long as we have music, darling."

"Yes." It was true in a way he could vaguely understand.

"Do what you must do," she told him. "I will be here for what will happen. But let this time be enough for now."

They sat tight together in the darkness, in a mantle they

drew about them. The town came alive with voices and other sounds. They did not hear, being together.

The shop was lettered "Freygang's Photography." The corpse was stretched upon a board tilted against a sawhorse. Spade, the undertaker, had done a careful job and the light of the lamp shone directly upon it. Tim Coleman's face wore a waxen sheen; the bullet hole in his forehead was noticeable. Spot Freygang, who doubled as reporter for the *Enterprise*, was focusing his camera. He was thin as a pencil, clad in a bright red shirt and striped trousers.

Jabez Wall was intoning, "Comin' upon the boy like that layin' there dead, well, it was a shock. He looked so young and innocent. Little did we know."

"One of the Colemans. Oh my, oh my. And they were out to rob our friend Sam Jones. My, oh my," said Harrison Deal.

Dick Land leaned against the wall, disliking the strange mingled odors of the room. "Glad you toted him in. I don't dare leave town whilst his brothers are in jail."

"Ah, yes," said Wall. "They have friends."

"Them and the James Boys and Billy the Kid. Allus there's them that sees good in them. Damn if I know why," said the marshal.

"Romance," said Harrison Deal. "Robin Hood."

"Never heard of no robbers in hoods around here," said Land. "Know all about the Kid. A snivelin' young fool. Come east to Silver City with his ma. Never was any good. The lies started about him after he stabbed a man and run off to Mexico."

"A backshootin' coward," said Wall. "The country's full of 'em. Best they should be wiped out. Sam Jones did the right thing. Shoot first, ask questions afterwards. That's the way the West was won. That's the way to keep it, more law. Better lawmen like you, Marshal."

Freygang set off his flash powder and the flare blinded

them all for the moment. He popped out from beneath the black hood and said, "I'll take a couple more. Can always sell 'em to the newspapers."

"You might take a picture of the marshal and Mr. Wall along with the—uh—corpse," Deal suggested.

Freygang wrinkled his long nose. "Uh, why not? Just stand over there, Mr. Wall. Like you're lookin' at Tim, thinkin' he deserved what he got."

Wall edged toward the body. He blinked, concealing distaste, faint alarm. He braced himself. Land shook his head, leaning against the wall. Freygang changed plates, altered his focus.

Harrison Deal prattled on, "You must know that Mr. Wall is a great force for good in the West. And now, with his purchase of the Long John Mine, he is about to bring great good to Sunrise. There will be more jobs and jobs mean prosperity for all."

Land murmured, "We doin' all right here for some time." No one heeded him.

"I will make notes for your editor, Freygang," said Deal. "Mr. Wall has vast interests up and down the land. The newspaper shall have a story. Make sure the pictures are good and clear. . . ."

Again the flash blasted; the odor of phosphorus became overpowering. Dick Land went to the door, opened it, and departed with a bandanna covering his nose and mouth.

Wall said, "Uh, that'll be enough." He handed a coin to Freygang. "Make the story good, son. We'll be needin' pictures as we go along with the mine."

"Thank you, Mr. Wall." Freygang closed the door behind them. He looked at the coin and saw that it was a four-bit piece. He grimaced and addressed the unseeing eyes of the dead man. "The bigger the cheaper. The hell with him. You're the one'll make me a few dollars."

On the street Grogan growled, "Hey, I got me a Mex whore 'cross town. You ain't needin' me."

"Go," said Wall. "There'll be no trouble tonight."

"If they lynch 'em, what the hell?" Grogan shrugged. "Tim looked better dead than alive, seemed like to me." He laughed and walked away.

Deal called after him, "Report at midnight, Grogan."

To Wall he whispered, "If there's no lynching we'll need to plan."

"Time enough. Now we go to the saloon and tell everybody how we're so glad the Colemans are under lock and key. Make it sound real true. You're good at that."

"I'm worn down to a nubbin, Jabez. All that riding," Deal complained.

"You think I'm fresh like a daisy? There's things have to be done at a certain time. A man has to ride whatever wave comes in. You mind the ocean? How the rollers come in and then there's the seventh and it's a big one, the prime one? That's the one to take to shore."

Harrison Deal was silent until they came under a cast-iron stanchion upon which was a carefully trimmed coal-oil lamp, a modern improvement of which Sunrise was proud. Then he asked, "What time is it, Jabez?"

Wall withdrew his watch, snapped open the gold hunting case. Then he hastily put it away. His voice was higher and thinner than ever. "Now, Harrison . . ."

"You brought it up. The waves. The sea. They were high indeed. The ship was rudderless but it floated. We were watching. Oh yes, we were ready."

"Damn it, Harrison. . . ."

"We could have saved it."

"You don't know that for fact."

"We had Captain Golden. He knew. Of course, he died soon after."

"Someday you're goin' to get yourself in trouble, rememberin' so much," Wall growled.

"I find it necessary to remember sometimes. As when you are flying too high, Jabez."

17

"I didn't kill the man."

"He was alive when we went aboard," Deal said.

"No mind. We needed money."

"We did, indeed. There was that deal you had to make. Eh? Just like now. Cash, you needed cash. When we went aboard the man was alive, I say. But you had to have the salvage."

"I said I didn't kill him."

"He died. You carry his watch."

"I'm warnin' you, Harrison . . ."

The voice of the lawyer was dry, cutting in. "I'm reminding you, Jabez. It's all written down. Always know that. It is in a safe place. If anything untoward should happen to me it will go to the authorities."

"You got no call to threaten me. We're partners. You're a rich man because of me, what I've done," Wall said.

"Starting with the salvage money. It was nip and tuck until then. Oh, we were in on it together. I'm an accessory. I could never inform upon you without facing indictment."

"We been through all that."

"You sometimes become headstrong, Jabez. As in the case at hand. The Colemans. I was against the Colemans," Deal reminded him.

"They were convenient. We needed that cash. It seemed easy to take it back. And I have other, uh, connections."

"Yes, and we must use them. The Colemans must never come to trial. They might talk if we desert them. We must plan with care. Jones—they call him 'Cemetery' and I do not like that cognomen. I sense an intelligence in the man. Also, he has a background in enforcing the law."

"We'll take care of Jones one way or t'other," Wall promised.

"Perhaps. Sooner or later. But with caution."

"Are you takin' over the business, Harrison?"

"As your legal counsel . . . and partner . . . I am warning you. The Colemans must be released or destroyed. We have influence in Santa Fe.''

"It won't work. The Colemans got too much agin them." Wall shook his head.

"Whatever we do, it must be done softly. Softly so far as we are concerned. It could all go down the drain, you know.''

"We got millions."

"Tied up tight. All that cash in the mine. And we will need much, much more. And your Colemans failed us today.''

"I know all that, Harrison." Wall was querulous. He touched the pocket that contained the watch. "The Colemans. You're right. I'll be thinkin'. We got a bit of time.''

"Not much time," the lawyer cautioned.

"We need cash. There'll be a way."

"I hope so."

"Let's go talk to people and tell our story. Let's get a woman. Be alive.''

They walked toward the El Sol Saloon. Harrison Deal said, "That watch. You should get rid of it. The man's name is engraved on it. Burr. Alexander Burr.''

"Now, Harrison, I prize this watch."

"Odd, isn't it?" Deal asked.

"What's odd about it?"

"Alexander Hamilton was shot and killed in a duel with Aaron Burr. Strange that a Burr should bear the name of a Hamilton.''

"Ah, just a coincidence or somethin'." But Wall was grimly silent as they went on their way.

When he was very young in Chicago he had wondered why his name, "Walner," had been the same as his mother's, why he did not have a father. He had been shining shoes when he learned in the streets that his mother was bringing home men for more than sociability. The boys called him "Bastard Joe." He was not strong enough to

19

fight them. His vengeance came from his ability to steal and lie without being caught.''

Opportunity hammered when a drunken friend of his mother's fell asleep and a wallet dropped from his pocket. Joe Walner was on the next train west, age sixteen, in full belief that any means was sufficient to the end and that money made the mare go.

The War Between the States had begun, a matter of no importance to him. He had found himself in Virginia City, Nevada, at a time of turbulence when men from the South lost influence and men of the North took over the politics. He had aligned himself with Jabez Firenzi, an Italian mine operator, fetching and learning. A chance came to steal a sack of gold from his employer just before that worthy died in a gunfight.

From then on it had been San Francisco, Denver, Cheyenne, any place he could invest and profit. Harrison Deal had been a young lawyer in Santa Fe trying to escape an unsavory past when the two had joined forces. They had prospered, but he who was now Jabez Wall had an overweening ambition to own everything upon which he could lay a hand. The result had been overextension and the matter of the foundering ship.

Again he touched the watch in his pocket, nearing the El Sol Saloon, his jaw hard. The man had been dying. He was certain of that. Captain Golden had not believed it, however. It had been a simple matter to shove Alexander Burr overboard—after emptying his money belt, of course. Captain Golden was a drunk, and he was soon dead on the Barbary Coast. Now only Harrison Deal knew what had happened.

Wall would have taken care of Deal before now had it not been for that document in a safe place in San Francisco. As it was, he must continue at status quo, using the legal tricks that Deal could manage, gritting his teeth at the sharing of money and power.

Nothing ever worked out in quite a perfect fashion. He flattered himself that he could make the best of a bad bargain. He was a successful businessman, he told himself; there was no margin for failure now.

2

Adam Burr was a large young man, too bulky for the long stagecoach ride to Sunrise. When he hit solid ground his knees were weak and cramps assaulted various parts of his body. He wore whipcord breeches, high laced boots, a light blue flannel shirt, and a flat-crowned felt hat, a costume advised by a New York salesman who professed to know about style in the Far West. He carried a carpetbag with changes of attire. Around his waist was an oilskin money belt containing some four thousand dollars, his entire fortune.

It was noontime and no shadows fell upon the stark outlines of the buildings that lined the main street. He turned in a slow circle and saw towering mountains north, south, east, and west. It was a wonderment how he had come to this place. The air was thin; its dry heat assailed him.

He located the bank, a hotel all of two stories high, a saloon. He was thirsty but decided to head first to the hotel, called Miner's Roost. The clerk wordlessly shoved a register at him, and he signed his name.

The clerk coughed and spoke. "New Jersey, is it? A far piece. It's siesta time. Town's nappin'. Take room four."

"I'd like to see a Mr. Solomon at the bank."

"Sol'll be around. Easy does it this time o' day." The clerk yawned and vanished from view.

The room was of good size. The bed was hard but clean.

There was a washstand with a pitcher of water and a cubby-hole for a chamber pot. Adam washed thoroughly and put on a clean shirt. He lay down for a half hour while his mind worked on his possible future.

He was twenty-one. He doted upon women and liquor. He had been three years at Princeton College before he had been forced to flee. His mother had disowned him and his father had been lost at sea and he did not have the slightest idea about himself, his talent, or lack of it. And he was making a new start.

He slept and awakened and went down into the street. He was hungry. He found a small restaurant where he was waited upon by a weary woman who brought steak and masked potatoes with gravy and apple pie. The food tasted flat but was filling.

The bank employed a teller and a plain girl who sat at a desk and wrote in a ledger. In Abe Solomon's back office he found the man he sought sitting with his feet up, reading a book. Adam asked, "Are you Mr. Solomon?"

The man lowered his feet and peered. He said, "I am. And you are Adam Burr."

Adam was immediately relieved that he was expected. "Yes, sir."

"I had a letter. A long letter from my dear old friend Jacob Wisberg. You have distinguished ancestry, no?"

"Aaron Burr was my great-uncle. If that's distinguished."

"A strange genius, he was. Your father was Alexander Burr. Yes. You killed a man."

"He came at me with a knife." Adam shivered, remembering.

"Women. Whiskey." Solomon shook his head, sighing. "Ah, youth."

"The woman was willing. I didn't know she was sister to the townie. Princetonians and townies are always at odds, y' see. He had this big knife . . ."

"You said. Your mother now. She disinherited you."

Adam took a deep breath. "Yes. Mother. I'd rather not
. . . I have four thousand dollars to deposit in your bank."

"You are maybe your father's son?" The voice was
kindly, the smile gentle. "So said Jake Wisberg in his letter.
A good letter. So, Adam Burr, this is a good town. Not
every person good, that cannot be. Mostly good. There are
women and men, some poor, some well off. There are dogs
and children. Sometimes there are cloudbursts scary, believe me. All people come together—Indians, Mexicanos,
Nigras also. You want a new life? This is a new world."

"I must try it," Adam said.

"It will try you. Death comes early and sudden to the
unwary. You will notice I am the oldest man in Sunrise. The
law, it is loose. A marshal. A circuit judge. From the outside, new, one Jabez Wall." Solomon peered at Adam.

"Jabez Wall? Yes, I remember the name."

"Jake Wisberg mentioned him, no? It was a good, long
letter from Jake. Wall is here with a lawyer, one Harrison
Deal. A tricky pair, I fear."

"My father's ship foundered, they told me. He went
down with it off San Francisco somewhere. It's all vague,
sir. Jabez Wall, he claimed salvage."

"Him I do not trust. Nor his mealymouthed lawyer."

"I'll keep my eyes open," Adam promised.

"And your ears. Right now there are outlaws in the jail.
Brought in by Sam Jones. A good man, Sam Jones."

"That's exciting. Outlaws. Back east we read about
them."

"Reading and seeing, two different things. For the
young, exciting. For me, worrisome."

Adam produced his money. "If I can deposit this with
you?"

"Always glad to get a new customer. You have money to
live on? It's expensive here, no?"

"More so than back home."

"Hard to get supplies up through the passes, over the

24

mountains. No manufacturing here. Not yet. You come back, talk to me. Any friend of Jake Wisberg.'' Solomon wrote a receipt. ''Move slow and be careful.''

''Thank you for your time, sir.''

Adam went back into the street. Now the sun was shining on the mountains to the east. Shimmering beauty was reflected from pyrites and other deposits. At noon it had been still, sullen. Now the town was bathed in beauty. It was a place of varied moods, he thought, walking toward the El Sol Saloon. Already he was feeling a tug, he thought, a relationship with this strange, wild place.

Inside the El Sol it was cool and dim, a pleasant escape from the lingering siesta time. Few moved on the streets. Sam Jones stood at the bar, four ounces of whiskey before him.

There was a long mirror, reflecting a row of shining bottles against the wall behind the bar. Two ceiling chandeliers hung high. The piano, a polished upright, was ensconced in a corner. In the rear were poker tables, unoccupied at present. Clean sawdust, brass spittoons, decorated the floor. Shaky, the bartender, wore a clean apron high on his ample middle and sported a handlebar mustache. Shaky had a nervous tic, which disappeared when he was pouring. He stood at the far end of the bar, polishing glass. The El Sol had pride in itself.

The doors swung open and Adam Burr entered, blinking from the sunlight, peering. Four men at a table looked back at him. Sam Jones scanned him from the corner of his eye. The young man was very big and very wide, they all noted. He was blond and blue-eyed, and when he walked, he walked tall. He was also one-hundred-and-one-percent tenderfoot.

He took a place four feet from Sam and put a coin on the bar. ''May I have a drink?''

Shaky came slowly, concealing a hardmouthed grin. "And what may you be drinkin', sir, please?"

"Whiskey and a beer chaser."

Shaky looked at the coin. It was gold. He picked it up and bit it. He nodded and put a bottle of beer, a mug, a bottle of whiskey, and a shot glass in front of the young man. He went to the cash drawer and took out a handful of silver, brought it back, and carefully deposited it on the mahogany. He concealed his shaking hands by folding them under his apron and asked, "Stranger here, ain't you?"

"Got in just before noon." Adam tossed down the whiskey, reached for the beer. He choked. He gasped. He fought for air. He tilted the bottle and drank the beer without pouring it into the mug. He said, "Woosh!"

"Little strong for you?" Shaky asked.

"Back home we drink mostly applejack. Smooth." Adam spoke with difficulty.

"Reckon you won't want any more of it, then."

"Leave the bottle," said Adam. "Just give me another beer and a little time."

Silence fell upon the El Sol. Adam leaned on his elbows and looked around. He took a sip of a second whiskey. He addressed Sam Jones. "Hot out there, you know?"

"Yup." Sam was regarding his reflection in the mirror.

"You live here?"

"Off and on."

"My name's Adam Burr."

"Sam Jones."

"Oh. Mr. Solomon at the bank was speaking of you. He said nice things about you."

"Friend of Sol's?" Sam asked.

"Well, a friend of a friend. I mean Mr. Wisberg back in New York sent me to Mr. Solomon. I've never been west before."

"I see."

"They thought . . . I mean, I am to try to find a job of

26

some sort. Here. In the West.'' Adam was babbling; there was something disconcerting about the man, the atmosphere.

The stillness descended again. The four men were talking in undertones, a drone of voices indistinguishable as to content. Shaky polished; Sam stood nursing his glass.

Adam said, ''Say, will you have a drink on me?''

''No, thanks,'' said Sam.

''Oh. Sorry.''

''Just havin' one.''

''That's okay.''

Now the voices at the table rose and a man called, ''Sam. Can y' spare a minute?''

Sam finished his drink and walked toward them. He was wearing his gun tied low and was not as much at ease as he seemed. At the table were Mayor Wagner, hay and grain; Frank Nixon, general store; Morgan King, mining; and Tex Tillus, rancher. They constituted the Council of Sunrise. All were on the lean side, tanned, prosperous.

Mayor Wagner said, ''Sam, we got word someone stole the cannon up at Santa Rita. You mind the old cannon?''

''Yup.''

''They also stole a can o' powder.''

''Mean business, don't they?''

''It's got to be the Pitmans,'' said Tex Tillus. ''Rob Pitman, he was in the army. They been seen around and about in the hills.''

''Most likely,'' Sam agreed.

''The Colemans been in the hoosegow for a week. The judge ain't due for three, four days. And Sam, Dick Land is gettin' along. Donkey, he's just a boy. We're beginnin' to worry,'' the mayor said.

''Dick's worried. Town's worried. Don't do a bit o' good,'' said Sam.

''We figure you might help.''

''Just how?''

"Well . . ." The mayor scowled. "You brought the Colemans in. You . . . I dunno, Sam. We're plain worried."

"You said that."

"That damn Freygang kid, he's been writin' stories about how slow everything moves. How the town's feedin' the prisoners on tax money. How the judge and the whole territory needs more law."

"He's right," Sam said flatly.

"It ain't helpin' any. The Colemans sayin' you murdered Tim."

"They say."

"Well, we know different. But if the Pitmans hook up with the Colemans some way . . ."

"What way?"

"I dunno," said the mayor helplessly. "It's just . . ."

"You're worried?"

"Oh, hell, Sam. People look to us for every doggone little thing."

"Can't help you," said Sam. "You can't do anything until somethin' happens."

It was like it was a cue. A tremendous explosion out in the town shattered the early-afternoon peace. The four men at the table started, interfered with Sam Jones. Adam Burr ran for the door.

Sam tore himself loose and interposed his body between the doorway and the men with the speed of a large panther. They fell over him.

Shots poured into the El Sol Saloon. Sam said, "Low! Keep your heads down and crawl."

They all, in great haste, obeyed. Lead whizzed over their bodies as they rolled away from the door. Sam had his revolver in his hand. He rose to a crouching position at the window, peering, removing his hat, venturing a further look. The others produced weapons, all but Adam Burr.

Sam said, "Easy does it. I reckoned they'd know we were in here. They got too much know-how."

There were shouts. The hooves of horses pounded. A girl screamed. Dogs barked furiously to the sky. Sam moved to the shattered door. He peered, thrust his gun forward, fired five fast shots.

The sound of horses diminished. Sam ran into the street. It was deserted except for a forlorn figure lying in front of the jail. Donkey Donovan reeled toward it, holding a smoking shotgun, bleeding from a head wound. In the middle of the street stood a cannon. The front of the jailhouse showed a gaping hole.

Donkey croaked, "The Colemans. Somebody busted us up and broke 'em out."

Sam knelt beside Dick Land. A small man with a black bag came with rapid, short paces to join them. People came from all directions to form a circle. The councilmen and Adam Burr were in the foreground, staring, disbelieving.

The man with the black bag was Dr. Bader. He looked up at Donkey Donovan and said, "Son, your boss man is in bad shape."

"Oh, hell and damnation. He was in his office. I was in the cells. They blasted us all to hell. Oh, God in heaven, Dick!" Tears ran down Donkey's cheeks.

"Easy does it," said Sam. "Guns and horses. On the double."

They moved fast, every able man in town. They were formed up in short order. Sam looked them over. He spied Adam Burr on a livery stable black. "Where you goin' without a gun?"

"Wherever you men go."

"What good can you do?"

"Maybe none. But I can ride. I have two hands." They were big, strong hands, unsullied by labor.

"No time to argufy," said Sam.

Abe Porter, a big, aggressive ranch foreman, said, "Git the greenhorn outa this. We got trouble enough."

"Just ride," said Sam. "They got a good start."

They rode out. The road led toward the far hills. The prints were easy to follow. Three Colemans, Pitman and his bunch, maybe a dozen men, Sam Jones thought. They all knew the country; they were all hardened; they were all desperate; they were all experienced in this kind of business. It was a futile chase, he reckoned, but it had to be made. Custom demanded it; the posse was an institution.

Soon the prints veered from the dusty road. Leading toward the foothills was a rising shelf of loose shale.

"Porter," said Sam, "ride ahead and make sure they turned off here."

"You want I should ride into an ambush?"

"I want to know if this is a trick."

"Send the stinkin' tenderfoot. He ain't no use."

Adam Burr said, "Sir, I object to 'stinkin'.' You want to get down from the horse and try me?"

"No time for that," said Sam. "Porter, ride on or go back to town."

Porter hesitated, glaring at Adam Burr. "Aw, bullcrap," he said, and rode ahead on the errand assigned to him.

The posse rode up the edge of shale to where a stand of trees barred the way. Sam got down from his dun horse and said, "I better make a pasear."

Adam Burr dismounted. "My boots are better on the ground. May I come along?"

Sam hesitated, then said, "Why not?"

They left the posse and climbed. The tenderfoot was a better walker than the horseman. They moved through underbrush among the trees, climbing. Sam did not try to make speed. They were soon out of sight of the riders below. Sam had a rifle in his hands. They came to a clump of brush, a leaning tree. There were signs of the escapees which Sam examined, fingering a horse dropping.

"Warm," he said. "They came this way. Watch out above."

They climbed among fallen boulders half as big as a house. Sam went ahead, looking upward for hidden guns. Adam followed, more preoccupied with the immediate surroundings.

There was a hint of motion from behind one of the huge hunks of rock. Adam saw it first and leaped to the left of Sam. Three bodies erupted, emitting high, keening yells. They were short men and they carried knives. One fired a shot from an old musket. It went wild.

Adam caught the nearest figure with a full swing of his right fist. Sam tripped and brought the rifle around as he fell, landing the stock on the neck of a second attacker.

Adam grabbed the wrist of the third, who threatened with a curved, shining blade. A moment of the past flashed through Adam's head, the man in New Jersey with the knife. He seized the wrist of this one and swung him. He kicked hard at the groin and the man groaned in deep anguish.

Sam was looking for further trouble. Adam followed on his heels. Far off above there was the echo of a gunshot. Sam said, "Whoa, steady."

They surveyed the fallen trio. They were young; they were copper-skinned. They wore leggins and loincloths. There were red bands around their heads.

Sam said, "These here are your first Apaches."

Two of them crawled upward toward the boulders, leaving the musket where it had fallen. One of them was quite still, his head at an odd angle.

Sam said, "Let 'em go." He examined the prone figure. "Afraid I broke his damn neck. Didn't aim to do that. Just young braves out to count a coup."

"A coo?" Adam asked.

"Yup. Like a white man's scalp, that's big medicine. Just touchin' you and gettin' away scot-free, that ain't shabby."

"Any white person?"

"Ain't no persons exceptin' them. They call themselves 'the people.' We ain't people to them. Funny. There's folks back there don't think Indians are people. Evens out, don't it?" Sam found himself talking more easily with this wide-eyed greenhorn that was his custom.

"It sounds rather crazy."

"Lots of craziness hereabouts." Again there was a gun fired above them. Sam toed the dead Indian. "But I ain't crazy enough to follow the Pitmans and the Colemans when they got us outnumbered and also have high gun."

"The posse?" Adam looked down below them.

"Too late. Too far behind. They'll cool off. Posses are always in hot blood."

"What must we do about the dead man, there?"

"We leave him. The other braves will come back for him. Part of what they believe. They might be lookin' for us, too. You mind that."

"Oh, I'll mind it."

Sam said, "You're mighty quick. Give you a gun and you'd probably do to take along."

"I don't know much about guns."

"You might learn."

"Well, I was always kind of quick." Adam hesitated, then said, "You see, I killed a man. With my hands. That's why I'm here. Mr. Solomon knows."

Sam was starting slowly back down the slope.

"Fella need killin'?" he asked.

"I truly don't know. He came at me with a knife. Scared me as much as anything, I guess."

"So you scragged him."

"Scragged. Yes, I guess so." Adam nodded slowly.

"Nothin' wrong with that. Him with a knife."

"The law didn't quite agree. There was his sister, you see. She was involved."

"Oh." There was a pause. "What kinda gal was this sister?"

"Well, she was for it."

"Then what the hell? Best you buy a gun. See me when we got some time. Sudden fella like you, you'll need a gun."

They had come down to the road. The posse was dismounted, lounging, waiting for Sam. Porter had rejoined them, assured that the outlaws had indeed headed into the hills. The sun was brilliant and the dust stirred in a quondam breeze.

Mayor Wagner asked, "Any sign?"

"They're clean gone up yonder," said Sam. "Apaches in the woods. No use tryin' to go up there."

Wagner said, "Nothin' to do but go back to town and organize a real party."

"It'll take a long time," said Sam. "And there's Dick Land to think about."

"We all set a heap o' store in Dick," the mayor agreed.

They were turning to their mounts when Adam Burr said, "Just a moment, please."

They stopped and stared at him. Sam sighed. He had a good notion as to what was going to happen.

Adam pointed at Porter. "I believe the word was 'stinkin'.' Maybe you'd like to retract?"

"I don't retract nothin' for no pulin' greenhorn," said Porter. "You just git on your plug and forget it."

"You won't apologize?" Adam asked.

"Oh, for goshsake." Porter took a step away, then swung back. He let go with a roundhouse right swing.

Adam caught the blow on his forearm. He struck out straight from the shoulder. The big cowman went down as if shot.

Sam said, "Okay, that's enough o' that. Porter, he'll kill you if you keep at him."

Porter said, "Lucky punch!" and rose, charging.

Adam hit him three times in the body and once on the jaw. This time Porter stretched out with a silly grin on his face, sound asleep.

Sam said, "Now look what you went and done. We'll have to waste water on him."

"Well, he did call me stinkin'," said Adam.

Someone emptied a canteen on Porter's face. He blinked his eyes and sat up. "What happened?"

"You should've seen Burr here against some Apaches up on the hill," said Sam. "He didn't stink and he wasn't useless."

Porter pulled himself erect. "Okay, he ain't useless." He staggered to his horse, grabbing the stirrup. "He just may be partly the hind end of a mule. I got no argument, no more."

Adam was flabbergasted for a moment. Sam watched him, a tiny grin showing. Then the hard line of the tender-foot's jaw softened. He said, "I'm for making friends." He went to Porter and extended a hand. "Okay?"

"You don't stink after all." Porter accepted the hand, straightened, rubbed his chin, and climbed aboard his horse. Sam shrugged.

They all mounted and rode back to town, silent, each with his own serious thoughts. They were tanned, seamy-faced from exposure to the elements, even the townsmen. None appeared to be past forty years of age. Their horses were tough and well trained.

Adam rode beside Sam Jones. He said, "Back home you couldn't gather a bunch like this in a month of trying."

"You reckon?"

"What will happen next?"

"A confabulation." Sam was sober-faced now, thinking of Dick Land. He had known the lawman for years; they had hunted and fished together. The older man had often given first shot at a running deer to the young Sam. There were few of his kind left; he was the Old West personified. Sam fell into silence for the time it took to get back to Sunrise.

Once in town, Mayor Wagner went directly to the telegraph office to spread the news that the Colemans had escaped and were presumed to have joined the Pitman gang. The posse broke up, but the councilors headed in a body for the El Sol Saloon.

Sam made for an adobe building on the edge of town which housed the hospital. Adam Burr tagged along, respecting the solemnity of the occasion. Dr. Bader met them at the door, reeking of alcohol but articulate.

"You just about have time, Sam. They got his lung. Can't do anything for him."

Sam removed his hat, baring wavy brown hair, which lay close to his scalp. Adam followed him into the room where Dick Land lay, his breath catching in a heaving chest. The marshal's face was wan, the lines of age deeply etched. He lifted one hand toward Sam.

"Friend . . . I seen 'em . . ."

"Don't talk, Dick."

"Gotta talk . . . Man don't cash in his chips every day . . . do we now?" His voice grew a bit stronger. "It was Rob Pitman and them . . . Damn cannon, what a stunt . . . That bunch means big trouble, Sam."

"Forget 'em. You got a family anywhere, Dick?"

"Nope . . . all gone or forgotten . . . Did that bunch make the mountains? Pitman knows them mountains like a book. . . . Had too good a start, didn't they?"

"Yup. Take it easy, Dick." Sam's voice was soft.

"Don't put the blame on Donkey. . . . It was too quick, real sneaky . . . my fault . . . Hell to get old, Sam."

"Never mind all that. Just take it easy."

"Howsome ever. We seen plenty good men go over. Leastways, I got my boots off." Land coughed up red blood. He tried to rise up from the pillow, reaching for Sam. He was smiling when he dropped back, his hand in Sam's.

"Hell," Sam said.

"Too bad," said Dr. Bader. "A good man."

"With his boots off," Sam repeated. He gently disengaged his hand and bent to close the eyes of the dead marshal. "Take care of everything, Doc. Send the bill to me."

They walked out of the hospital. Adam could find no words. They repaired to the El Sol Saloon. The bartender put out the whiskey bottle.

"Dick went over, huh?" Shaky asked.

"Yup." Sam poured and passed the bottle to Adam. "He went good."

From the back of the saloon Mayor Wagner called, "Sam. Got to palaver."

"Dick just left us," said Sam.

"I figured. Got to talk, Sam."

"Some other time." Sam was looking at the mirror but not seeing his reflection. His mind was turned inward; death was invading his thoughts. The Apache hadn't mattered, it had seemed. Now all the deaths mattered, including that of Tim Coleman. And all the deaths to come mattered, those of good men and bad that were certain to occur.

Sounds from the piano flowed into the dim room. Renee was wearing a black gown, her white hands moving with grace and surety.

Adam whispered, "Why, that's Handel. The dirge."

Sam half turned. Then he finished his drink, poured another, and walked slowly to the piano.

Shaky said, "Shh. She plays weird but good."

Adam helped himself to another drink, paid. Sam stood close beside Renee, listening, drinking it in. It altered his mood, yet did not dim his sense of loss, his distrust of the near future. She looked up at him and shook her head ever so slightly and he nodded in response, warmed by their communication.

Men came into the saloon and tiptoed, remaining near the front of the establishment. Adam moved slowly down to the far end, nearest to the piano. It was a requiem for Dick Land, he realized. No more respect had ever been shown in the greatest cathedrals. Twilight fell and Shaky went noiselessly to the chandeliers to light them. No one spoke until the music stopped and Renee bowed her head, hands clasped, and Sam moved closer to her.

There was a long wait, then she said, "Come, Sam."

They went to the table where the councilors waited. The men scrambled to get a chair for the lady. She sat down and said, "Make your speech, Mayor."

"Well, it's about what will happen now. The Pitman gang and the Colemans. Up in some hole Pitman's got above the mines. No way to get at 'em. They could hold off an army. But they won't stay up there, will they?"

Sam shook his head. All the men in the bar were listening; none spoke.

Wagner said, "You killed Tim Coleman. That means they'll be after you like a pack of hounds."

"I'll handle it." Sam's voice spelled indifference.

"More'n that. They'll be on this town. They'll come down again like today. The bank. You've got money in the bank, Sam. Abe Solomon's your friend. You want to see Sol go down, too?"

"Not the point."

"Sam, we want you to take over Dick's job." The mayor put a shiny silver star on the table.

"No."

"Come on. You made your strike here. You been a lawman. You know the job."

"Never said I liked it."

They had come to an impasse. Renee sat expressionless. Adam Burr felt suspense, the need for a sign.

Young Donkey Donovan crept from the people at the bar to stand across from Sam. There were tears on his cheeks. He said, "Sam, I feel like it's my fault. I want to make it up a bit, somehow, someway."

"Wasn't your fault. Dick said so," Sam told him.

"I shoulda been readier. Somethin'. I shoulda done somethin'."

Wagner inhaled, exhaled, began again. "Sam, we purely need you. There's nobody else."

"Just don't want the job."

"Hell . . . 'Scuse me, Renee. . . . We know you don't want it. Don't need it. We're askin' you, please. We need you bad." The mayor extended the shining badge.

There was a long pause. Now Sam was staring at Renee. She smiled sadly, inclined her head a fraction of an inch, then raised her brows, questioning. Sam shook himself like a wet dog. His face came alive, hard, filled with foreboding. "If I take it, I got my own ways."

"Any damn . . . 'Scuse me, Renee. . . . way you want it!" Wagner said.

"I don't take orders good. I run her as she lays."

"That's fine with us."

"I don't walk streets nor jail drunks."

"If you want Donkey, he can do that."

"I want him."

Donkey Donovan's back straightened. "Before God, Mr. Jones, I'll do anything . . . anything."

"Just your job'll do," said Sam kindly. He looked at Wagner. "Might want some other things."

"A hundred a month and fines."

"No wages."

"Oh, come on, Sam."

"Pay it to Donkey. They coulda killed him, too, y' know. I'll take expenses. I'm doin' this for Dick Land. And only until the Colemans and the Pitman bunch are wiped out." Sam picked up the badge and Renee leaned to take it from him and pin it to his vest. "Money don't count. I ain't for sale now nor any other time."

A high voice in the background said, "Well said, sir." Wall said. "We all grieve for the brave marshal. It would be my pleasure to buy drinks for the house on the occasion of the naming of the new lawman.'' Jabez Wall was waving his arms at the bar.

There were men who responded. Harrison Deal, close beside his partner, was putting down money. Adam Burr remained where he stood. Renee went to the piano and played a mazurka. The mood lightened at once. Sam beckoned and Adam joined him near Renee.

''Not drinking with Jabez Wall?'' she asked.

Adam started. ''That's him? Jabez Wall?''

''You know something about him?''

''I want to know.''

Renee asked Sam, ''May I meet your young friend? I mean, may I have something to call him?''

''Uh . . . Adam Burr . . . Renee Hart.''

''So nice,'' she said. ''From the East.''

''New Jersey,'' Adam told her.

''Ah, yes. Princeton, I should imagine.''

''That's right.''

''Lovely town. I played a concert there once,'' she said; then a veil settled over her face and she looked away. *She's looking into the past,* Sam thought.

A young girl came on dancing feet to join them. She was blond, her hair in braids. Her eyes were a contrasting dark brown. She was no more than five feet tall. She exuded vitality, curiosity, a straightforward challenge to the world. She was very pretty.

''What's goin' on?'' she demanded. ''Poor Dick Land. I been sleepin' the day away.'' She peered at Sam. What you doin' wearing that damn badge? Has everybody gone loco?''

Sam said, ''This here is Sally McLaine. Adam Burr. Take it easy, Sal. Part of the world is mad all of the time.''

Sally was looking Adam up and down. ''A tenderfoot

as I live and breathe. Don't get many like you these days.''

"I'm sorry about that," said Adam. "Pretty girls should have a choice in men."

"Talks fancy. Interestin'," she said. "I aim to go east someday. Sing in the big theaters."

"If you last that long." There was meaning in Sam's voice, a warning.

"I may last longer than you." She flipped a finger at his marshal's badge and addressed Renee. "Hey, keep on playin' a lively tune. Maybe I can hustle up a dollar or two dancin' with all these gents."

Renee smiled, her composure restored. She changed key and played. It was Mozart, Adam realized. She played it with a swinging lilt that altered the light genius of the composer and brought it alive, vigorous.

The girl pirouetted to the men at the bar. One of them detached himself, grabbed her, and began whirling her around. Adam looked questioningly at Sam.

"Good gal. Lost her folks. Has to work."

"A dance hall girl?"

"Don't get yourself mixed up. Maybe she ain't exactly pure. But she's straight folks."

"No offense intended," Adam said with haste. "Just that—well, we all read about honky-tonk girls. You know, those stories."

"Gal is left alone," said Sam. "What can she do? Marry a cowhand and raise a passel of kids and die young, that's what. Or maybe she can sew a seam, make dresses. Or wait tables. Sal, she can sing. Good, Renee says. Meantime she has to eat and pay her board."

"I understand," Adam said. But he did not, of course. He watched the girl as she accepted a coin from the first man, then went to another, her tiny feet tripping and kicking. She was enjoying herself; that was evident. When the man lowered his hand to pull her closer, she slapped it away, and still she laughed and danced.

It was suppertime now. Renee stopped playing, looked at a thin gold watch pinned to her chest. Jabez Wall and Harrison Deal had paid the bill and departed. The customers began exiting the El Sol. Sally came back to them, shaking her head.

"He wanted me to go with him and stay. All night. For two dollars. Imagine!"

Renee said, "Sally, you come upstairs with me."

The girl blinked her eyes, seemed about to be defiant, then went meekly in the wake of the statuesque figure of the other woman.

Sam drawled, "Renee gives lessons in ladying."

"Does this place have . . . rooms upstairs?"

"No, friend."

"I just have a lot to learn."

"Look and listen." The young man has a way about him, Sam thought. "What about Jabez Wall?"

"He salvaged my father's ship when it went down off San Francisco. Mr. Wisberg said there was something missing, something strange in the story they gave out."

"I wouldn't be amazed."

"Wall is big on bein' law-abiding," said Adam. "Right?"

Sam thought a moment, then said, "I got a suspicion he tried to have me bushwhacked and robbed. You got a suspicion regardin' your pa. If we both keep quiet and, like I say, look and listen, we may learn something."

"Agreed. Now can I buy you a drink?"

They were still at the bar when the women came downstairs. There was little change in Renee, but Sally's braids were wound around her head and she wore—instead of tight jeans and a man's shirt—a demure nut-brown dress that swept the floor. She curtsied and simpered, "Are you gentlemen ready to escort us ladies to dinnah?"

She's irresistible, Adam thought. Cute as a bug was the

Jersey expression. A church bell rang. The street was almost deserted. Sunrise had subsided for the moment.

But Dick Land lay dead and the hills were full of outlaws.

3

The mesa lay between mountain and desert, high enough and far enough from the nearest mountainside to be out of range of the most powerful rifle. They had built a single road to its top and erected canvas shelters for protection against the elements. Rob Pitman sat on an empty dynamite case and ruled like a czar.

He was a medium-sized man who dressed in dark clothing and wore a black sombrero. His face was thin, his mustache full. He had slim hands that were never quite still. His eyes were deep-set, piercing. He was as dangerous as an adder.

He said, "Okay. We sprung you. Now what can you do for us?"

Frank Coleman answered for his brothers. "Whatever you got in mind, Rob. What we want is Jones."

"Revenge. If it fits a plan. What we want is enough money to leave this damn place," Pitman said.

"It looks mighty good to us after where we been."

"Leave this country," Pitman went on, unheeding. "Get to where money counts, where a man can live and breathe and enjoy. Don't you ever enjoy?"

"Why, sure. Liquor, women, music for dancin', lots of things," said Frank, somewhat bewildered. "What more?"

Pitman regarded him contemplatively. "What, indeed?" Certainly none of his own men had higher notions. They

43

were a hard-bitten crew: Sandstorm, Montana, Snakehead, Cortez, the black giant Absolom. He never knew nor wanted to know their real names. He had gathered them one by one, knowing their strengths and their weaknesses. He had not a whit of concern for them nor for the Colemans; they were all grist to his mill.

He had founded a small army and his fort was impregnable. He had horses; he had ammunition; he had dynamite. He had a large amount of paper money cannily secreted in the lining of a saddlebag. He needed one more big strike before he left his minions to their own devices. He had a strongbox they all knew about which was their share of plunder and to which they were welcome, only because he did not want to have any or all of them on his trail when he vanished from their ken.

Actually, he considered himself an honorable man according to his lights. He had a Calvinist background; as a child he had rebelled against the strict discipline and been terribly punished by cold, harsh parents. He had run away before graduating from school into a world of dire reality and had learned to swim with the tide, choosing criminal ways, which came natural to him. Early in the West he had acquired all the tricks of the outlaw trail as though born to them. He had made his name a byword; he had never been apprehended; he felt safe against primitive law. He was neither too proud nor too humble; he was master of his followers and none defied him and lived.

He said, "The town, Sunrise. What have you learned?"

"Jones had a lotta cash from Jabez Wall. He must've put it in the bank. There's a new feller in town; he put more money with old Solomon. There's mine money and cow money, lots of it in that there bank.

"The law?"

"Nothin'. Dick Land, he went down when you busted us out. Purely nothin'."

"Excepting Cemetery Jones."

"Yeah. Him." Frank Coleman scowled. "He killed our brother."

"I know." Pitman knew a lot of things that he kept to himself. "I'll think on it."

"Jabez Wall, he hired us," Frank Coleman said.

"He did, did he?"

"Well, him and that slick lawyer. They might have somethin' worthwhile. They bought the mine from Jones."

"Did they, now?" Pitman knew about that also.

The sun was drooping behind the mountaintop to the west. There were clouds that gave a purple shadow. A slight breeze cooled the mesa. Someone started a fire. Absolom got out his banjo and began to play "Buffalo Gals." Rough voices raised the lyrics.

Frank Coleman said, "It's right nice up here. You got some vittles?"

"Plenty. Just go ahead, boys, meet the other men, enjoy yourselves. I'll be talking to you."

Pitman sat alone, pondering. He had just enough of them now, not too many. A raid—a quick, well-organized raid—might do it, he surmised. Still, there was the other problem. As dusk took over to the sound of music, he waited for full dark and the signal from below. The men brought him food: chicken, baked potatoes, fresh bread from the farm a half day's ride into the valley which he had purchased and rented to a faithful Mexican couple.

It was when he had been buying the farm from a bank that had foreclosed upon it that he had met Jabez Wall. Wall had been posing as a land speculator and the two men had recognized the rascality in each other on sight. You can fool some of the people some of the time, the outlaw mused, and regretted that the mantle of sin lay upon him so clearly as to be spotted by such as Wall. Still, everything had its use, and Wall's interest in Sunrise might pay off. He had looked up Wall's holdings and made an estimate prior to the man's purchase of the mine from Cemetery Jones. Pitman had put two and two together and decided he knew enough to do business with the crooked businessman and his sly lawyer.

He ate slowly, enjoying the food. Darkness fell abruptly as it did in that part of the country. Soon there was the flare of a torch far below. His surefooted cayuse was saddled and ready. He spoke to no one as he mounted and rode down the narrow path he and his men had hewn from the mesa.

4

The town fell back into its normal ways, but not without unease beneath the surface. Tempers were on edge. All passers through were looked upon with suspicion. Every arrival of the stage was the center of attraction. Donkey Donovan did the police duties wearing two guns and carrying a sawed-off shotgun, a "greener." There was confusion even in the El Sol Saloon, ordinarily a quiet establishment as compared to the two other places, the Cobre and the joint owned by Rafferty. The dancing in the El Sol was more hectic, a way of letting off steam, and Sally McLaine was profiting thereby.

Jabez Wall and Harrison Deal were absent on "a business trip." Abe Solomon watched it all with sober mien, shaking his head, concerned about his clientele, who were all his friends. Only Renee Hart seemed serene, playing her music, oblivious.

But behind the marshal's office-jailhouse Sam Jones was saying, "We've got the holster right for your reach. Now you got to learn to get the damn gun out and aim it. You aim like you're pointin' your finger. Don't believe all that bulldung about sightin' a revolver."

Adam squinted in the afternoon sun. "There's a lot to learn. Furthermore, I don't know if I could actually shoot a man."

"A man comes at you, believe me, you'll shoot. And

never forget: Don't draw that thing unless you mean to fire it. And always aim to get your man between the neck and the hips. The head's a hard target, and any other place, he'll shoot back."

"I don't see how a man can be hit by a forty-four or forty-five bullet and not go into shock."

"Oh, they do that, all right. But somehow they get off one or two unless you hit 'em right."

"Reflex action." Adam nodded.

"Whatever. Now try that draw again."

Adam assumed the position. He reached for the butt of the Colt in its cutdown holster—a Cemetery Jones Special. He got it out with celerity.

"You got the quick hands," Sam told him. "You got the good eye. You don't need target practice no more. Just get a bit faster."

Adam had been at it for a week. He had, as Sam noted, proved a natural shot with the short gun. His rifle work had not been quite so productive, but he had good coordination. He was sweating now in his new clothing: Levi's, a light wool shirt, a vest; in fact, the same costume worn by Sam Jones, including soft cowboy boots, but with a modified heel. Adam had tried the high heel and found he could not manage without wobbling like a girl. Like Sally McLaine walking down to the El Sol.

Donkey Donovan came around the corner of the jailhouse and said lugubriously, "Fella came in on the stage. Jeez, Sam. Said his name was Convy. Said he was lookin' for you."

"Hell," said Sam. "Convy, huh?"

"Wearin' two guns, Sam."

"Sure." Sam turned to Adam. "This happens. It's damn stupid, but it happens once in a great while."

Donkey said, "I told him he couldn't wear the guns, like you said. He laughed nasty at me."

"Sure he did. Headed for Rafferty's?" Sam asked.

"How'd you know?"

"He wouldn't find backin' in the El Sol. He can make his brag in Rafferty's and get by."

Adam asked nervously, "Is this a shoot-out? Like I've heard about back east?"

"That's what Convy wants. He's a fast-fingered, no-good galoot goes around for such nonsense. Dime novel stuff," Sam said.

"He'd kill you just for fun?"

"For his reputation. He's one of *them*. There ain't many around, never were. But here's one come to town."

"What are you going to do?" Adam asked.

"Oblige the bastid, of course," said Sam.

"When he asked he called you 'Cemetery,' " said Donkey. "Cemetery Jones, he said."

"Yup." Sam adjusted his belt and grinned. "They always want to get it straight. If he downs me he'll go to Spot Freygang and try to have his picture took with my corpus."

"I can't believe it," said Adam.

"You better had. Like I said, it don't happen often. But when it does, you better believe." Sam walked leisurely around the jail. Adam and Donkey followed, neither quite sure of the procedure.

"Couldn't the three of us just arrest him? Get him in cross fire?" Adam suggested.

"We could." Sam's eyes actually changed color. They became colder than ice. "I don't do business thataway."

He touched the brim of his hat and walked down Main Street. There were plenty of witnesses. Even Abe Solomon came into the sunlight blinking, his mouth drawn down at the corners in disapproval. Sam saw them all: Shaky, Wagner and the councilmen, wives and children. The dogs lay low, sensing the fear of their owners. Convy's brags had permeated Sunrise.

Aware of Adam and Donkey a respectful ten paces behind him, Sam sauntered toward Rafferty's, at the north end of the street. It was an event out of the past. It had been a long while since this foolish pattern had risen to disturb his equanimity. The occasion with the Colemans had been another matter altogether. They had waylaid him and Tim had lost his head. Tim would have killed him. That was like a war.

This was different in his mind. This was a challenge to his station in life, to his masculinity. Convy was just another young fellow gone wrong, living off a secondhand reputation. He had killed a few men in saloons; he had forced duels on men who had desired them and on those who had not. He was a vermin in the burgeoning West, a scourge of decent, law-abiding folks. Sam did not think deeply on men like Convy. He became a machine walking an invisible line, an ethical line having naught to do with morals. That he wore a badge was unimportant.

Furthermore, he knew there was an element in Sunrise, as in every community, that resented the law, indeed resented authority of any sort. Envy is a curse, he had learned. Pride goeth before a fall, he reminded himself. But he lived in pride; he strode with pride. His pace increased as he neared Rafferty's, his steps became longer.

The saloon was dingy, but there were windows that provided plenty of light. Sam came swiftly through the doors. Men scrambled to keep out of line of possible fire. Convy stood at the bar, a whiskey in his hand. He spun, catlike, both hands spread.

"Cemetery Jones," he said. He was a tall, thin man with an aquiline nose and a slightly undershot jaw. He had narrow-set eyes and a thin mustache. He wore range clothing, city-style. He spied Adam and Donkey and went on. "You need backin', huh, Cemetery?"

There was a full moment of complete silence. Then Sam said, "Draw, you stupid bastid."

The hands dropped, very fast.

Sam stepped forward, drew the Colt with the speed of lightning, and slammed one shot. He slid the gun back into place and looked around the bar, looked at Rafferty. He never glanced at the dying man on the floor. He said, "Get Doc Bader and take care of this trash."

Rafferty, a burly man with a full beard, said, "Whatever you say, Marshal."

The customers came to stare at the supine figure. The bullet had taken Convy full in the chest. His guns were barely cleared from their holsters. Someone said, "Migawd, he never knew what the hell hit him."

"He knew," Sam said coldly. "They always know when it's too late. If another comes along you might tell him that."

He turned and walked out. Adam and Donkey followed in his wake. They almost ran down Sally McLaine, who was waving in triumph to the cautious citizens who were awaiting the outcome. She fell into step with Adam as they made their way toward the El Sol.

She said, "Sam got him quick, huh?"

"Yes," said Adam. His mind was still reeling with the suddenness of it.

Donkey said, "Never seed nothin' like it. Don't expect many ever did."

Sally said, "Why you think they call him Cemetery?"

"You never seen him do it," Donkey told her.

"I saw it this time. Underneath the swingin' doors."

Adam stared. "You were watching?"

"You think I'd miss it? I want to see it all. I want to see the elephant."

"Uh—well, you're a girl."

"You noted?" She smiled at him. "Next thing you'll be askin' me to dance."

Adam could not find a reply. They went into the El Sol. Mayor Wagner and the councilman and others were present. Abe Solomon was nearest the entrance. Shaky was putting out a bottle and three glasses and bottles of beer. Sam nodded thanks, shook his head, and went up the stairs.

Shaky caressed his mustache with trembling fingers. "How did it go?"

Donkey said, "Sam done it nice and easy."

Mayor Wagner said, "Alone, by gum. That's his way. I wish he'd be more careful."

Donkey said, "You want to tell him?"

"No. Nor anybody else. I just wish."

"Because you need him," Adam said.

"Sure. Sam's been around. He knows how it is," the mayor replied.

Donkey said, "He's set in his ways. He's one hiyu man."

"Who said different?" Abe Solomon spoke. "Each unto his own, no? If a man has a way of doing, that he must follow. We all want law and order, no? What Sam did might not be law. It was order." He waved a hand and walked out of the saloon.

Doc Bader entered, poured whiskey, drank it, poured another. "Thirsty damn business. Gunshot wounds. Messy."

"Is the coot alive?" asked Shaky.

"Hell, no. Right in the heart. The bum had a hundred dollars on him. Imagine that. He coulda had a real bust on a hundred before he croaked."

"A hundred?" Mayor Wagner scowled. "Just one hundred?"

"Right. Gold and bills. It'll bury him."

"He coulda been hired," said Wagner. "Damn! Sam's got to know about this."

Shaky said, "If you bother Sam right now you'll be one sorry hombre."

"Bother him? I ain't goin' near him till he comes down," the mayor agreed.

They all went to the bar and passed the bottle.

Renee was waiting in her room, reading a book at her window. When Sam entered she carefully marked her place and remained silent, her hands folded in her lap. He un-buckled his gunbelt and placed it on the dresser. The room was furnished comfortably in earth colors, two deep chairs, a large bed, a long closet behind a draw curtain, a thick carpet, papered walls. There was a cabinet loaded with sheet music and a bookcase entirely filled.

Sam said, "It ain't what I want to do."

Through the open window came the shrill voice of a boy. "The marshal done it! He downed him with one shot!"

Renee said, "You didn't have to do it. You had the two young men."

"That's what Adam said. I didn't have to do it."

"But, you answered, that is not your way."

"There's a difference, Renee."

"You could have jailed him."

"And when he got out?" he asked.

"Put him on the stage."

"There's a stage every day."

She sighed deeply. "The West."

"Yes. The West. My country."

"Your country."

"But you adopted it. Why?"

She withdrew into a shell he recognized. "It matters not," she said. "I see it differently than you. I see what Abe Solomon wants. I share his vision."

"Law and order. It's comin'. Meanwhile . . . there's a Convy here and there. He asked to be snuffed out."

"And you obliged him. When will it stop?"

"Not as long as I'm alive."

"We're not talking on the same level, Sam."

"Right."

"Sooner or later they'll get you when you're not looking."

"Yup." He nodded.

"There must be a solution."

"I ain't lookin' for solutions. They keep comin'—and the

53

Colemans and Pitman will be comin'. I keep tryin' to give 'em answers. I don't know any other way.''

"And you never will." Now she rose and went to him and touched him. "I know you don't want to kill anyone. I know you are a product of time, place, and circumstance. And God help me, I love you."

He was rigid. "Yup. It ain't enough, is it?"

"Enough for now."

"There's goin' to be hell to pay. I smell it. I'm into it. I took the damn badge."

"You think there's going to be trouble. Are you looking for it?" She immediately altered her mood. Her arm went around him. "You're not. Where you are there is always some kind of trouble. And Sam, I know you're abiding by your beliefs, by what you are and who you are."

"Like I said, it ain't enough."

"It's enough for me."

"Maybe now, it's enough."

Her voice deepened. "Sam. Take it as it goes."

"There's no other way."

"You must do what must be done." She withdrew, feeling the stiffness in him. "I can't help you."

"I never ran to booze. I never ran to a preacher, not any man. Now I'm runnin' to a woman. It won't go down."

"It's not a weakness, Sam."

"It's just not my way."

Now she smiled. "Cemetery Jones."

"Yup." He suddenly rose and buckled on his gunbelt. She said, "Go and do what you must. I'll be here."

"Damn it, you deserve better."

"Ha! It's not for you to say what is better or worse for me. Go and get yourself straight in your head."

He hesitated, then kissed her briefly and left. She sat back down in her chair but did not resume her book. She thought of the past, and her chin became firm and her eyes as hard as Sam's had been.

* * *

Sam went directly to the livery stable, where he saddled the dun horse, slung on his saddlebags and blanket, and rode down to the general store. He purchased cold victuals; he did not intend to build a fire. There was fire enough in him. He was no longer able to wait for invasion of Sunrise. He needed to know whence the danger would come.

He was packing the food into his saddlebag when he saw Jabez Wall and Harrison Deal across the street. He thought that they were startled to see him alive. However, he could be wrong, he supposed. He had nothing definite to tell him otherwise.

When the two men started toward him he lifted a hand, shook his head, and rode out northward. He had a definite destination in mind. He rode to the place in the road where the Pitman-Coleman gang had disappeared. He put the dun on the steep trail and went slowly to where he had stopped Adam Burr from going further. There was sign to show the Apaches had picked up their dead young brave.

There was also plain trail leading upward. The dun footed it with care crossing a rocky ravine, then with acceleration climbed upward.

It was at the top of this wooded foothill that Sam could see the mesa. The day was waning and a swirl of smoke ascended to a cloudless sky. It was wispy smoke that could be controlled only by man. Sam trailed the reins of the dun and took from his bedroll a pair of moccasins, which he exchanged for his high-heeled riding boots. Donning them, he sat beneath a tree and watched the mesa. When his eyes were adjusted to the light and shadow he made out the road ascending to its flat top.

He folded himself into a comfortable position and sat like a lizard in the waning sunlight, his hat tilted over his brow, his extraordinarily sharp, adaptable eyes scanning the surroundings. Time went away, meaning nothing. He pried open a can of tomatoes to refresh himself, ate a cracker, washed it down with water from his canteen. It was a time for caution, a time for patience.

At twilight a figure appeared astride a cayuse. Down the road it came until he could distinguish Jake Coleman, complete with rifle in its scabbard, revolvers belted.. In a moment Jake was followed by another horseman. In the declining light Sam could barely make out their movements, but he knew they were sentinels of the early watch, that Pitman was not one to be caught napping, that the impregnability of the mesa top depended upon vigilance. It was also possible that there was an alternative retreat from the stronghold. Safe as it was from assault, its occupants could be starved out by a siege of determined men.

Sam debated with himself. He had traced the beasts to their lair. Alone he was powerless against them. He had not enough facts to call upon the governor to send troops or raise militia—he knew the reluctance of politicians to create controversy of any sort. He had no stomach for cutting off either of the outlaw guards; arresting one of them would not suit his purpose, in any case. It was best, he thought, to savor the fact that he knew of the bastion, to store the knowledge and use it when the time came.

Further, he was chary of another killing. He could speak of necessity, but he could not in his heart condone the shooting of a human being. He needed time alone in the open, a small purifying of the soul.

He mounted the dun in complete darkness. The moon was behind a clump of clouds. A rain would be uncomfortable despite his slicker. He rode around the mesa on the north side, going slowly, allowing the horse to find its footing and in some small way the goal. It was late when he came to the terrain he knew, adjacent to the Long John Mine, into the arroyo where he had evaded the trap laid by the Colemans.

He loosened the girth on his saddle and the dun drank thirstily from the stream that caroled its way down the mountain. He stretched out, his head on a clump of moss, hat brim down. He should have felt at home here. He should have been at ease. He should not have been wondering what Renee was doing, and Adam and the girl Sally McLaine and Abe Solomon and young Donkey Donovan. Was he putting down roots? In a town? It seemed impossible; he was an outdoor man.

He sat up. He remained cross-legged, putting his mind to the situation that affected all these people who ran through his thoughts. He owed a debt. He was not entirely certain how this had come to pass, but he knew it was true. He went to the dun and cinched up and mounted. He rode back around the mesa, the notion of spending the night outdoors fading. He came to a safe place and dismounted.

He could move like an Indian in his moccasins. The two sentinels were asleep. He was not surprised. Men living outside the law lacked discipline. They resented assigned duty in the off season, in dull times.

Sam carried his rifle while climbing the outlaw trail, wary of loose stones, of potholes. He was a wraith in the deep night. He came to the perimeter of the mesa. He lay quiet, listening, holding his breath when there was the slightest movement of man or beast.

The fires had died down. There were a couple of tents, but most of the company slept in blankets circled around banked fires. He counted them, making no attempt to identify individuals in the darkness. He brazenly stuck his head into the tents. He needed to know how many. It occurred to him that he could seek a spot where he would be protected, start firing, and decimate the gang one by one.

He actually grinned as he began the descent. Cemetery Jones, alone, thinking about wholesale murder atop a mesa—something that was not his style no matter the cause. He touched the silver badge, which was really nickel-plated. A strange life, he thought, a very strange life indeed for a man wealthy enough to go to any far place he desired.

He came to the glade where he had left the dun horse. It was missing. He whistled and was answered with a shot. He fell flat, nose pointing in the direction the shot had come from. He fired three times in quick succession. Now there was all hell to pay; the sentries would be awakened, he was afoot, and there were enemies between him and town.

He ran, doubled over, toward the area of the gunman. He stumbled and almost fell. The dun whinnied. He knew he had fallen over a body. A quick examination proved it to be half-naked, an Indian. Remembering the Apache youths, he knew they had intended this time to score a coup by stealing his horse, a great feat in their tribal custom. He ran forward among some trees and found the dun giving harsh trouble to an Indian attempting to mount. Like most cayuses the dun was somewhat of a one-man horse.

Sam swung the barrel of the rifle at the head of the Apache. Then he leaped into the saddle and headed for town. Luckily the horse was rested and both knew the way. Atop the mesa the outlaws would be awake and coming pell-mell to ascertain the trouble. He hoped the young Indian could somehow escape.

He need not have gone to the top of the mesa. He could have guessed the strength of the gang. He always had to be dead certain, though; it was part of his system of survival. Much risked, little gained, he admitted. Still, it was his way.

The mesa was clearly impregnable to attack in force. Pitman was clever. The Colemans were tough and bad all through and burning with desire for revenge against him. There was truly nothing he could do but await circumstance. It would take an army to starve them out, and there was no evidence that could call out such a force.

It was a time for patience, of which he had little, of which indeed there was little in the people of the West. It had come down upon Sam to make decisions that were alien to his own character. He slowed the pace of the dun when he was certain there was no pursuit. He had much to pore over, and he wondered whether it would all come together in Sunrise.

5

It was quiet in the El Sol Saloon. Mayor Wagner was drinking rather more than usual, glowering alone in a corner. There was the usual crowd, decent citizens conversing, consuming quantities of beer. Renee played her music, but no one was dancing. Adam sat at a table near the piano, enjoying Renee but feeling somewhat alone without Sam Jones.

Sally McLaine came down the stairs in a short dress with a low neckline, her hair done high, looking older than her years. She went to the piano and said, "Let's try 'em with a song."

Renee said, "It's not time for loud music, dear." She ran her fingers slowly over the keys. Sally shrugged, put a hand on the piano, and faced the audience.

"Alas, my love, you do me wrong to treat me so discourteously, and I have loved you so long . . . delighting in your company . . . Greensleeves was all my joy, Greensleeves was my delight, Greensleeves was my heart of gold . . . And who . . . but Lady Greensleeves?"

She had a full voice, bigger than Adam would have thought. There was a haunting quality in her, in the ballad.

There was a stillness afterward, a tribute to her. Renee smiled and went into "Buffalo Gals" and Sally took it and swung it and went down the line of men at the bar and they pressed coins on her.

Renee went into Bach then, stopped midnote, and came and sat with Adam. Sally paused in the middle of a solo dance step, stared a moment, then joined them, the coins twisted into an oversized kerchief.

Renee said, "That's enough."

"Why? I got to make a livin'," said the girl.

"Ah, yes. But tonight . . . I don't know."

Adam said, "Maybe because Sam is gone."

"Sam ain't the whole of the world," said Sally. "All this scary business about outlaws, that's what's got everybody down."

They were silent. The talk in the saloon was a murmur. Sally was right, Adam thought. Looking at her, he thought of the proper girls back home, the sort the Princeton boys courted. She was much more alive, much prettier.

Renee said abruptly, "Why don't you two take a walk?"

"A walk?" Sally's brows went up.

"Get some fresh air. Talk. Be acquainted."

Adam said, "Why, that's a splendid idea."

"A walk?" Sally repeated.

"Yes, dear," said Renee. She arose to return to the piano. "Boys and girls often take walks."

Adam got to his feet. "Please?"

"Well . . . all right. But I'll lose money," Sally told him.

Adam said, "I'll pay."

Again silence fell. Then Sally said, "No. I couldn't take money for walkin'."

She laughed and they went out the rear door and into the alley. They turned onto Main Street and strolled. It was later than they thought. And they found themselves talking— about their lives, so different yet so alike. He was a fugitive;

she was alone. There was one big difference, he pointed out. She had a goal.

"Your voice is very good. It needs training, but it is there."

"Trainin'? You're funnin' me."

"No. Voice training is necessary in order to make a success of singing in the East."

"You know a lot of things like that, don't you? I had a schoolteacher once. He knew things. He knew how to grab a girl, too."

He said, "With your looks and training you could make it."

"I got to get the money to keep me for a year. That's a lot of money."

"Yes." He hesitated, then said gently, "There must be a better way."

He felt her withdraw. "You think I'm just a whore, don't you?" she asked.

"No. I think . . . I think you're a girl who has no other choice."

"But you, you're from a different place in life."

"No. I'm going to be a westerner. I'm learning things that are not in books. I think you're a fine girl."

She stopped. She stared at him in the dark night. "You do? Honest to Injun?"

"I don't lie about things like that. Sam thinks you're a fine girl. So does Renee. Their opinions are worth a lot."

"I . . . I don't want to go to bed with men. I don't like it."

He took a deep breath. "It was over a girl that I got in trouble. She did . . . like it. Her brother came at me and I killed him. Am I any better than you?"

She said flatly, "I don't reckon anyone is better than me. I'm what I am for now. Not forever. For now."

They walked without speaking, thoughts whirling in their

heads. They came further than they had intended. They found themselves in the light reflected from Rafferty's bar. Figures emerged, shouting, brawling.

Harp Grogan had hold of a man in each hand. He howled and banged them together. Their heads cracked and they went down.

"I told ye I could whip any two men in the house," shouted the big man. "When I want somethin' I take it."

He beat his chest and his eyes fell upon Sally and Adam.

"Hi, there! The little whore from the fancy joint, eh? Right now I'll take her."

He made a lunge. Adam stepped inside the wide, grasping arms. He struck once, twice at the middle of the big man's body.

Grogan folded over. Sally stepped forward. She dug a heel into his instep, then brought both hands down on the back of the neck of the roaring figure. Grogan staggered, then came erect. Up went his hands in the posture of a prizefighter.

"I'll kill ye both!" He was frothing at the mouth.

Adam danced inside again. He took a forearm alongside the head as he busied his quick hands. He landed one to the breadbasket, two to the side of the jaw, right, left again to the body. Grogan snarled and kicked.

Adam went backward, arms wide. Grogan hit him on the jaw. Adam reeled, covered up. Grogan swung a long-armed right fist.

Sally squealed, "Duck, Adam, duck!" Two men had grabbed her, holding her, laughing. The crowd from Rafferty's grew. It was late at night for peaceful citizens to be about, but a crowd of rowdies soon surrounded the combatants.

Adam ducked. He was dizzy. He stepped to the left, then the right as Grogan bore in. He blocked a punch. He countered with a long left. The bigger man was a sucker for a jab,

Adam thought dimly, sticking, sticking, trying to recover his bearings. The big man could also hit a ton, he knew.

Grogan crouched, his right fist making a small circle. There was blood on his face and he licked at a broken lip, his eyes fiery red. He was ready to deliver his knockout punch. Adam circled.

Grogan came in and let it go, a roundhouse. Adam again stepped inside. He struck with his left, hooking it. He caught Grogan in the throat. This time he lifted a knee to defend against the kick. At the same time he dealt a terrific right to the big man's breastbone.

Grogan choked out a mighty oath. His arms sank. Adam went forward, seeking to finish it.

A hanger-on at Rafferty's stuck out a foot. Adam stumbled. His arms windmilled as he tried to maintain balance. Someone shoved him at Grogan. He was off balance. Grogan hit him with the right. Adam went down full-length. Sally screamed. Grogan aimed a heavy boot at Adam's head, a lethal attempt, a kick that could kill. Sally screamed again.

Adam managed to roll over. He was on all fours as Grogan kept coming.

The voice of Sam Jones said, "That'll do it."

Grogan stopped, his head swinging about. Adam scrambled out of range and said hoarsely, "I can handle this."

"No fightin' in the streets. That's my law," said Sam without emotion.

"The big bastid grabbed me," Sally yelled. "Two of these bums have been holdin' me."

Sam said, "We'll talk on that later. Grogan."

"I'll kill him anytime," said Grogan hoarsely. "Anytime, anyplace."

"Into Rafferty's." Sam spoke with cold emphasis.

Grogan hesitated, then walked toward the saloon. Someone in the crowd called, "It was a fair fight."

"No kind of fightin' in public is fair around here," said Sam.

There was some laughter, some grumbling, more than enough rebellion held in check.

Adam found Sally at his side. His head swam; his knuckles were bruised. He felt somewhat foolish with Sam's hard eye upon him. They turned back toward the El Sol.

Sally asked, "You hurt bad? I saw them trip you up. You sure you're okay?"

"My feelings are hurt. Nobody ever knocked me down before." Adam grinned at her. "You certainly did your best."

"If they hadn't held me . . ."

"You might have been hurt."

Now she was shy. "Well. We were gettin' along, you know? Like good friends, talkin' and all."

"You've a lot of friends in town."

"No. Renee. Sam. Maybe Shaky." She shook her head. "A girl like me, she don't have friends."

"Well, you can call me friend," Adam said.

"You don't dance with me. You just . . . look, sometimes."

"I'm new here. I'm learning the ways." He did not know how to say that it irked him to see her take money for a dance, that always in the back of his mind were the trips upstairs at the hotel. Front of the mind, he corrected himself.

"I know." She understood too well. They entered the El Sol in silence. There was only one candelabrum lighted. There were three customers: Sam, just entered, and at the near end of the bar, Jabez Wall and Harrison Deal. Renee was playing softly, something Adam did not recognize, something with a somber meaning.

Sam asked, "So now tell me."

When they had finished he turned to Wall and Deal. "This hombre Grogan, he works for you."

Wall said, "At times. At times."

"Yup. When you think you need muscle," Sam said.

"It's a rough country, Marshal. We are not men of arms."

"Yup. So you tell Grogan, one more time like this and he goes into the pokey."

"Of course. Certainly. You're absolutely right."

Deal asked, "Buy you a nightcap, folks?"

"Nope," Sam replied

Wall took out his watch, hiding it in his hand, opened it, and glanced at the face. "Time to retire. Good night, all."

When they had gone Sam said, "Just how drunk was Grogan?"

"Hard to tell. He could punch straight enough," said Adam.

"Funny he should pull a whangdoodle like that just when those two are back in town."

"We shouldn't have walked that far at night," Adam admitted.

"Yup. Still and all. We got the Colemans up with Pitman and a tight bunch of gunners in a place where they feel safe as grizzlies in a cave. We got Wall and Deal down here. I'll bet a lot they hired the Colemans to waylay me when I came down from the mine. I haven't a smidgen of evidence. I only got my hunch. Now, if Pitman broke out the Colemans, why?"

"No love lost among them people," said Shaky.

"They brought down a cannon. Somethin' brand new to me. Lots of trouble. Lots of guts," said Sam.

"They killed Dick Land," said Renee, her hands still, the music ended.

"Yes. They killed a good man, a good friend." Sam picked up the nightcap poured by Shaky.

Renee came to the bar and sipped at a small brandy. "Your reasoning is sound, Sam. We all know there will be an attack on the town. That's why you're here. I suggest that their first move will be to eliminate you."

"Could be."

"So you went out alone, right to their doorstep." She shook her head.

"How else to locate them, know what they might be up to?"

"How else indeed?" She smiled. "Cemetery Jones."

"What was that you said one time? Them that lives by the sword dies by the sword?"

"Hey," said Shaky. "Time to close up."

Adam said suddenly, "I could whip that Grogan."

"Sticks in the craw, does it?" Sam nodded. "I know how it feels."

Sally said, "He can do it."

Renee looked thoughtful. "I've been trying to raise some money for the people on the other side of town. Poor children who need. Maybe it would clear the air, provide funds."

"Like what?" asked Shaky. "Like a prizefight?"

"Whoa," said Sam. "A crowd might leave an opening for Pitman."

"Not if we laid a trap," said Renee.

Sam shoved back his hat. "Sometimes, woman, you sound like a sharp man."

"Oh, thank you, sir." She laughed. "Think about it."

Adam said, "Any day."

"He can do it," Sally said again.

Sam shrugged. "While I stable my horse, why don't you two see if you can get back safe to the hotel?"

They walked close together again, the two youngsters. The lobby of the hotel was deserted, lit by a single lantern. She went up a step, stopped, her head almost on a level with Adam's. She said, "Was I too fresh?"

67

"Not at all." She was lovely—and vulnerable in the soft light.

"We are . . . friends?"

"Absolutely."

Her natural aplomb had deserted her. "I can get by with singin' and dancin'. No savin' money. But I could live okay."

"I'd like that a lot." He had not before experienced the emotion he was now feeling.

"Fresh start?" There was a world of meaning in her words.

"Yes."

She stuck out a hand. He took it. She said, "I never had a fella near my age for a pal before."

"I never had a girl for a friend before."

"But you had plenty of gals." She was back to normal.

"I think I see what you mean. I agree."

"Even Steven," she said.

He would not have thought of such a deal ever before, but now it was different—this new life, this new country, and far from least this tough-minded, straightforward girl looking him in the eye. "Right!"

She leaned forward swiftly and kissed him on the cheek, then ran up the stairs, giggling, showing thin ankles and legs.

In the doorway Sam witnessed this, saw Adam climb slowly, thoughtfully upward. For the first time that day he felt himself grinning from ear to ear. He tiptoed after them and quietly went into his own room next to Adam's. Town life, he thought, was softening him up.

Then he thought of his pasear earlier that night. He was not weary, but he felt exhausted. Too much was resting on his shoulders; his mind was too full of possible dangers. This town, this Sunrise, was beginning to stretch, to be what a community should be. It would be tragic indeed if disaster

68

should fall upon it. And he knew that only his wits and his experience and his guns stood in the way.

He knew that as surely as he knew his name. And the name he hated, "Cemetery Jones."

6

The back room of Rafferty's Saloon had only a rear door. Casually surveyed, it could be a storeroom. Rafferty, bearded and red-eyed, rolled around through the adjacent alley and slid back the cleverly built entrance. Jabez Wall and Harrison Deal followed closely in his footsteps.

The room was lighted by a lantern. It contained four double-decked bunks, crowded but habitable, a long bench, and one hard chair. In the chair sat Rob Pitman, dressed in black, hat cocked back, expressionless. It was two o'clock in the morning and the moon was still blocked behind the hovering, dense clouds.

Wall said, "Ah, Pitman, I see you didn't believe me."

"No honor among thieves," said Pitman.

Rafferty said, "He come at me strong. I hadda let him in."

"Quite proper," said Harrison Deal. "We had informed him of this hideout."

"Here is where you can plant your men. I told you that," said Wall.

"And have somebody squeal?" Pitman sneered.

"Damn few know about this room," said Rafferty. "I hid a few people here from time to time. Like the Colemans."

"And I had to bust the Colemans out," said Pitman.

"And their brother got his and they ain't too crazy about you, none of you."

"What in hell could I do?" demanded Rafferty. "I hid 'em. They went up the mountain, and Jones was too smart and quick for 'em."

"Jones," said Wall. "Something has got to be done about Jones."

"And the tenderfoot," said Rafferty. "Grogan woulda taken care of him if Jones hadn't come into it."

"Grogan is helpful," said Wall. "Grogan will now be even more than ready."

"Grogan is a horse's patootie," said Pitman. "Muscle don't count for a hell of a lot. Brains is what we need."

"If we time it out with a mine payroll," said Wall, "there's a fortune in this town. You can have everything but the cash I need to develop the Long John Mine."

"We talked about that," said Pitman. "Thing is, we get the blame; you stay clear and get what you want. They'll be after us."

"We'll do everything to hold them up," Wall promised.

"You can't do doodley squat about anything while Cemetery Jones is alive."

There fell a long silence.

Wall demanded, "Can't we hire a gun? Is there no one?"

"You tried it with Convy," Pitman reminded them. "He's as fast as the others. Dumb move, bringing in Convy. Jones is smart. Maybe smarter than any of us thought. The only way we're going to take over this town is with him in his own cemetery."

"Cross fire," said Rafferty. "You plant the guns in here, take him by surprise."

"Taking Jones by surprise won't do it. Man like him's got eyes in the back of his head."

Harrison Deal spoke for the first time. "The Colemans will do anything to get him."

"We need the Colemans," Pitman said. "You know

71

what it takes to do a town? You got to cover every angle. You got to have some of the town with you. People can spoil it with one lookout, and this town's already scared.''

"There's some don't cotton to Jones," said Rafferty. "I can handle them and still stay under cover.''

"You and Wall and Harrison. Staying under cover. That makes it twice as hard. A gang can ride in, ride out, split the take, and break up in several directions,'' said Pitman.

"You're a smart man,'' said Wall admiringly, fawning. "You tell us what's the best way.''

"The best way is to be lucky. Something happens that we don't start. Keep in close touch. Be ready. I'll be ready to hit when that time comes.'' Pitman went to the door. "I know every way in and out of this burg. I know every street, every alley, every building. You tell me when it's ripe and I'll do the rest.''

"But first we get Jones?'' Wall asked.

"I'll think on that. Cross fire? Maybe.'' Pitman nodded to Rafferty. "We can use this hideout.'' He paused. "What's your bit?''

Rafferty said, "The El Sol. I wanta be like the El Sol.''

Wall and Deal stared, perplexed. Pitman's smile was quirky.

Rafferty glared back at them. "Shaky ain't no better than me.''

Pitman said, "What he means is he wants enough money to have a place like the El Sol. Everybody wants somethin'. Nothin' wrong with that. If we blow down the town, why shouldn't Rafferty get what he wants?''

"We can't destroy the town,'' cried Wall. "I've got a stake here. All I need is ready cash. To take over the town. The bank. Build a mill for the Long John ore . . .''

Pitman interrupted, "Sure. We all want somethin' big. We mean to grab it. You mind the Northfield Raid?''

"That was different. That was stupid,'' said Wall.

"The James Brothers and the Youngers. They thought

they knew their business. Only the James boys got away. People died.''

"If we do it right . . ."

"We already killed a good man, Dick Land. If me or any of my men are caught, we hang. What about you three?"

"You won't be caught if we do it right."

"We got one advantage the James bunch didn't have. You people inside. But we got another thing Northfield didn't have. Sam Jones."

Wall said, "Well?"

"You can't handle him. No one man can handle him."

Pitman stood up. He crouched, made a lightning-fast draw of his gun that startled them all. The little grin again slid across his face. "He's quicker than that."

Deal said, "My God!"

"Faster than that?" Wall's eyes bugged.

"Convy was that quick," Pitman told them.

"You know Convy didn't clear his guns," said Wall.

"Certainly not. Jones got him straight on. You people been around this country a long time and you still don't know about a man like Cemetery Jones? He's a straight citizen. He's quiet; he tries to mind his own business. Seems like ordinary. But you put him in a tight spot and you got all hell, I mean all."

"Then it's got to be like Wild Bill Hickok got it. From behind," Wall said.

"You want to try that?"

"There's got to be some way."

"You go figure. You set it up. I'll bring the guns."

"But he's got friends to watch for him. The tenderfoot. Donkey Donovan. And, by God, the piano-playing woman and the dance hall girl."

Pitman laughed. "That's an army? Look, if you people can't rig something, the deal is off. Even with all my bunch I won't move until Jones is taken care of."

"You're afraid of him?" Wall asked.

73

For a moment it seemed Pitman would go into a rage. Then he said quietly, "I'm not afraid of any man. But I know what I can do. I can organize. I can plan and carry out. This is a thing that has to be done right or not at all. I don't aim to be a Younger, dead in the streets of Sunrise."

Rafferty had been gazing at first one, then the other of the trio. Now he said, "Harp Grogan."

"He's a drunken fool," said Pitman. "A thug."

"He's been—uh—helpful," said Wall.

"He's a mad dog about that tenderfoot. He'd kill him if he could," the bartender said.

"So?" Pitman asked.

"The tenderfoot's always hangin' around Jones. Supposin' Grogan went after him but grabbed Jones instead?" Rafferty suggested.

Pitman said, "Out of the mouths of . . . never mind. It's an idea."

"But that'd be murder and the town . . ." Wall stopped.

Pitman said, "A rifle. At a safe spot."

"Then why not a rifle anytime? Jones walks around town. Rides in and out of town," Wall said.

"With *his* rifle."

"If he's shot in the head . . ."

Pitman said, "Nobody is goin' to take that chance."

"Is this Jones a god, then?" demanded Harrison Deal. "Can no one eliminate him?"

"He's the devil," said Jabez Wall.

Rafferty said, "Ain't no man can't be got. I seen the best go down. Trouble is, man like Jones, there's others to take up. I see what Pitman means. I still say Grogan if it can be done right."

"Could be." Pitman rose. "We know what we want. Wall, you want your thirty-five thousand. Rafferty, you want enough to start a new joint—we can break up the El Sol durin' the fun. I take the mine payroll, whatever I can get. Understood?"

"Understood," said Jabez Wall.

Pitman eyed them. "A deal is a deal. Never mind honor. You people make a mistake—you don't stay under cover— you won't even live to see another day."

He was gone. He had the gift of nonappearance, of being there one minute and gone on the instant. There was not even the sound of the door closing. Outside the hoofbeats of his horse were muffled.

Into the stillness Rafferty said, "You heard him."

"I believe him," said Harrison Deal.

"No!" said Wall. "The man is no Cemetery Jones. He admits it."

"He's got the Colemans and the others," said Deal. "He's smart, Jabez, real smart. He'll take it all. You know he'll take it all."

"Nay," said Rafferty. "In this country a deal's a deal. I got customers that can help. But by Gawd we can't go against both Jones and Pitman. That's plain suicide."

"You're right," said Jabez Wall. He looked at his gold watch. "Best we break it up now."

Rafferty let them out one by one, watching, careful. Wall and Deal went separately to Main Street and thence to the hotel. They entered Wall's room and sat with their heads together, whispering.

"The main aim is to have the town," said Wall. "Stake Long John Mine. Take over the bank. Restore order after the raid."

"After Jones is dead there will still be people who are not for us," Deal reminded him.

"Then we must win them over. Petty cash will do it. No one has anything on us as of now."

"They're against Grogan."

"Grogan can be sacrificed. Let us think on what Rafferty proposed."

"But how do we arrange for the rifleman?"

"Pitman," Wall said.

"A difficult proposition, Jabez."

"It must be done."

"Allowed. We are not men of action. Therefore we must be men of acumen."

"And we are! We will prevail."

They sat bravely whispering. They had the force; they had the means. They needed only a plan, the proper plan.

It was a night for confabulation. Renee sat in her deep chair and said, "There are wheels within wheels if you are right about Jabez Wall."

"I'm right about him and his slimy lawyer," said Sam Jones. "I know about Pitman and the Colemans on top of the mesa. I'm right about that hundred dollars Convy had on him; he'd have spent it before comin' here if he hadn't picked it up here instead. I'm still nowhere."

"Forewarned is forearmed," she said.

"With what? Adam Burr, Donkey Donovan, and a scared-to-pieces town council." He sighed. "All that money in the bank and no place to go."

"You wouldn't have it any other way."

"Oh, yes I would. Think what you and me could do with that money."

"Spend it? Sam, you're not a man to settle down, not now, not ever. No, don't tell me about us. I know you. I love you the way you are. Just keep doing your best for Sunrise, for your friends."

"My best don't look too promisin' right this minute. They could lay a rifle bullet into me anytime they get smart enough. They could take this town over if they had the guts, the bottom, the brains."

"They could." She nodded, smiling. "They will try."

"Yup." Now he matched her smile. "Been there before, haven't I? Not so tight, maybe. But it goes down like it has before."

"You'll be there when it happens," she said.

"I aim to be there." He moved to her and she rose and they embraced. They were comfortable together, holding tight.

When he left an hour later he found Adam Burr sitting in the dark lobby of the hotel, legs outstretched, smoking a cigar. Sam asked, "You got somethin' on your mind besides Harp Grogan?"

"A lot."

Sam sat down. "So?"

"Work. I must find work."

"Yup. Satan always evil finds for idle hands to do. Someone told me that a long time ago."

"My mother. If she ever met you." Adam grimaced. "My mother is a hard lady, Sam. She never forgives. Not my father, not me. Tell me, is there any way I could learn what really happened with my father? And Jabez Wall?"

"It's possible. When this ringdang is over in Sunrise we might take a look."

"I want that. Sam?"

"Yup."

"Sally said she wouldn't go upstairs with a man ever again."

"She said that?"

"She . . . she kissed me. On the cheek."

"I be gum," said Sam solemnly. "She did so?"

"This is all so new to me. I . . . I like her a lot."

"Good notion."

"Imagine my mother and Sally. Whooee," mused Adam.

"Don't think on it. Now, about Grogan."

"He'll be after me, won't he?"

"Every minute." Sam shrugged. "Practice with that Colt. Walk on eggs. More'n Grogan will be after us."

"Because I'm your friend?"

77

"Partly. They'll be onto Donkey, too. Or anybody that could give trouble."

"When?" Adam asked.

"It's their move."

"Anytime, then?"

"It's like a small war, son. One move'll break it open."

"I see." Adam paused, then said, "The town's sitting on your shoulders."

"And it ain't comfortable. Now go to bed."

Rob Pitman did not ride far from his meeting with Jabez Wall and Harrison Deal and Rafferty. He made use of his ability to remain invisible and watched. He saw Sam Jones go to the hotel, waited until the light in his room was out. He waited to make certain that the town was surely asleep.

Then he rode to the rear of Abe Solomon's bank. From his saddlebag he took a dark lantern and a slender steel rod shaped with a flat end and a sharp end. He walked with great care to the rear door. It was a simple matter, given his skill and experience, to pry the door open. He stepped inside the bank and again was very still, not even a shadow in the office of Abe Solomon.

He struck a sulphur match and lit the lantern in one sudden move, working the shutter so that only a sliver of light showed. He went to the main portion of the bank and quickly rifled the cash drawers. There was not much money therein, but that did not matter to him. He went to the huge iron safe, which did contain cash and gold, and knelt. He examined it with great care.

Now he knew what it would take to blow it open. He had apprenticed in safe-cracking at one time in his career.

He next turned to the books. They were of no value beyond that they revealed the business of the customers of the institution; nevertheless, he made a bundle of them. He had no wish to destroy anything. He only wanted to throw a scare into Sunrise. He wanted to leave a mark. The town was already on edge, he was well aware. Upon learning that anyone could enter and rifle at will, there might well be a run on the bank, but this he doubted. The solid citizens would set up a watch, prepare a trap. And so long as he knew of the ways and means, he would know how to overcome the handicap. It was his method to always know what to expect. With the aid of Wall and Rafferty and the others he would be able to accumulate the knowledge he needed.

Now he went out the way he had entered. He scuffed his footprints one by one, going to the black horse with the money and the ledgers. He took his time putting it all into his saddlebags. Then he mounted and rode away to the fort above the mesa, well satisfied with the night's work, not believing in his allies, communing only with his own plans and desires.

7

Sam awakened with a start. It was six o'clock in the morning and there was a knocking on his door. He admitted Donkey Donovan.

"It's the bank," said the deputy. "Y' know how Abe sometimes gets there early. Well, somebody broke in."

Sam poured water in the basin and washed. "How much did they get?"

"Abe didn't say. He wants you."

They walked down Main Street. A few early birds were about. A farm wagon rolled into the general store loading platform.

Donkey said, "I started my rounds a little after five. Didn't have too much sleep. The baby had the colic."

"How's the wife?"

"Poorly since the baby took sick. The extra money you give us helps some. Doc Bader, he ain't much with babies."

"We'll think on that."

They came to the bank. Sam knew the vault hadn't been blown. He wondered. Solo bank robbers were a rarity in this part of the West.

Sol awaited them in his office. He spread his hands and said, "What can we do? A goniff breaks open the back door. He steals maybe a hundred dollars, some change."

"It don't appear sensible," said Sam. "A man could get shot for that little."

Sol said, "But he took the ledgers."

"Ah," said Sam. "That is a circumstance."

"Maybe to cause a run if I didn't have this." Sol produced a sheaf of foolscap. "Always in case of fire I keep double accounts, rough but correct, no? In the vault."

"He didn't monkey with the vault?"

"Not a mark on it."

Sam nodded. "Rob Pitman. His callin' card."

"So?"

"Just to let us know he's around. Donkey, you go over and get Adam."

Donkey departed. Sam sat down and put his feet on the desk. "Fella like Pitman, he's smarter than most. Young Burr, now, he's lookin' for work. College boy and all. Reckon we could put a cot in here."

"More help I don't need. However, a guard I could use, no? And maybe Adam could learn the business."

"A hundred a month ought to do it."

"If he learns well it could be more."

"No use spoilin' the young."

Sol asked, "This Pitman. He is the smart one?"

"He is that."

"He brought the cannon?"

"He did that." Sam thought of the cannon now sitting in the blacksmith shop. He made a mental note to keep it in mind.

"The Colemans and Pitman. They will come down like wolves upon a flock of sheep," said Sol.

"That's the general notion."

"Could we send for help? Money buys people."

"Trouble is, the people money buys can be as bad as the wolves," Sam said. "Reckon I shoulda had them put on a night deputy."

"It is not too late," said Sol. "No good horse has yet been stolen, so lock the stable door."

Adam Burr arrived. "What happened?"

They told him. Sam said, "You wanted a job. Know anything about bankin'?"

"I took a course. Double-entry bookkeeping, all that, in prep school."

Sol said, "Good! Hereabouts banking is people. They want you to take care of their money, pay a little interest. We buy mortgages, sometimes a bond. There's no big profit, but enough. It builds."

Sam said, "You'll sleep here. Save hotel money."

"And a hundred per month," added Sol.

Adam said, "Why, that's keen. I mean, maybe that's it for me." He was genuinely excited. "After all, I wouldn't make a top cowboy. Mayor Wagner offered me a job in the store, but somehow I couldn't make up my mind. This is just fine!"

"You sleep with your guns," said Sam.

"Oh. Yes, I see."

"Wouldn't be much time to hang around the El Sol." Sam permitted himself a grin. "On t'other hand, you might could entertain one gal at a time in the office here."

Adam blushed. "That'll work out."

"So it's settled," said Sol. "My teller and bookkeeper will have to know about the burglary. I trust them."

"Tell 'em to keep their mouths shut," said Sam. "Less said the sooner mended."

"They will be as the tomb."

Adam said, "I'll get my gear. Is there a closet?"

"There is," said Sol. "Yonder." He shook his head. "That we should come to this. Always it has been so peaceful."

"Storms come, storms go," said Sam. "This man Pitman, he's maybe too clever. Too much confidence. Do what must be done. I'll check back later."

He went out with Adam. They walked to the hotel. "Buy a bell. Hook it onto both doors, front and back. Sleep light, boy, sleep light," he warned.

Adam said, "I will feel as though I'm doing something, at least."

"Stay away from Grogan. Don't take on too much booze, not anytime."

"Right." Adam felt a wave of responsibility. "If I can learn the banking business . . . This is a huge opportunity."

"When they do come, it'll be to the bank. You can count on it."

Adam grinned at him. "You and me, Sam. Guardians of the town."

"I want to see Wagner."

Sam went up to finish his ablutions. He never felt right in town unless he was shaved and bathed. He came down and found the hay and grain establishment open. He went in and drew Mayor Wagner aside.

Sam said, "They're gettin' ready to make a break on us."

"How do you know?" Wagner was tight-lipped, nervous.

"Signs," said Sam. "I'm goin' out to look around. Pass the word quiet. Tell the right people. Remind 'em that the crowd around Rafferty's ain't to be trusted."

"I'm worried about that."

"You're damn right. Talk to only those we can trust."

Sam went down to the jail and selected a rifle. Donkey was checking the town. Sam waited until he could corner the deputy.

He said, "Mum's the word. You know anybody we could put on nights?"

Donkey considered. "There's Charlie Snodgrass. He's younger'n me, but he's honest and outa work. Got a gal he wants to marry. Mabel Graham. Dressmaker, she is. Miss Renee knows her, buys from her sometimes."

"Hire him. A hundred to start. Say nothin' about the bank. Just warn him there'll be trouble."

"Hell, Sam, every kid in town knows that."

"Good. You're in charge until I get back."

Sam walked down to the blacksmith on the edge of town. Andrew Holcomb was a squat man bulging with muscle. They exchanged greetings. Sam said, "That cannon. If it worked for them it'll work for us."

"For us? You funnin' me, Sam?"

"Put it in workin' order, whatever it needs. Oil the gear, the wheels. Get some powder and shot."

Holcomb scowled. "Sam, I got a wife and four kids. What's goin' to happen?"

"You figure it out. Pitman and the Colemans."

"Can't we do somethin' about 'em before they hit?"

"You think the governor would do anything?"

"That one? He wouldn't raise a finger until hell froze over," Holcomb said with disgust.

"You get the cannon in shape and keep a gun handy."

"It's hell, Sam, us with families. It's pure hell."

"Not until it happens," Sam told him.

He went to the livery stable and saddled up the dun. He was going on a bootless journey, he felt, but he had to be certain he was right. Every detail counted; it was all forming a pattern in his mind. He was trying to think like the outlaws. He was trying to decide what he would do if he wanted to take over a town and rob the bank and wherever else there was loot. He had never seen such a large operation take place. The James Brothers and the Youngers had attempted some part of such a scheme at Northfield, but the circumstances had been different. They had gone too far afield from their own territory, and it had been a stupid plan from the start.

Sam discounted his personal danger. He had known from the day he had killed Tim Coleman that the brothers would be on his trail. It was a matter of pride as well as vengeance with them. Joining Pitman had been the payoff. Together they were powerful.

He had no trouble picking up Pitman's trail once he was clear of town. Foreknowledge of the stronghold atop the mesa made it a matter of course. He had no notion of what to do about it except to make sure of his prey. He felt, however, that again he needed some time alone, away from the civilizing influence of Sunrise—and Renee. He had long since been aware that his thoughts were never very far away from the lady piano player from the East.

Far short of the mesa he rode through a stand of piñon and watched small creatures scurry from the fall of the nuts. He sat a moment under a clear sky, remembering the Apache youths and their attacks. He remembered a chief he had once befriended, one Jose Aragon, one of the few of the race who could be approached. Sam swung about to the west and again sought trail from approximately the last place he had seen the young braves.

He came to a tall old rock oak beside a stream. He stood on the saddle, reached a limb, and climbed. He was thirty feet off the ground when he saw movement in brush a hundred and fifty yards from the dun horse. He came down fast, skinning his shins and elbows.

He melted into the brush. There were only two of them this time. Their red headbands were bright in the sun dappling the floor of the clump of trees.

He waited until they were very close. The dun neighed and stomped a foot. The two Apaches came to capture their prize.

Sam stepped out with his revolver in his hand. "Just stay right there. I'm gettin' tired of you pesky kids. You get yourselves killed for nothin'."

They understood him well enough. They half raised their hands. Their black eyes gleamed like hard gems. They carried old rifles, which they dropped as they glared.

Sam said, "You walk me to your chief. You do it now or I swan to ginney I'll take your scalps instead."

He knew they spoke Spanish and that most of them understood basic English. "Scalps" got to them. They walked, leaving the ancient weapons behind. Sam leaned to pick them up. The Apaches had better guns, but the youths were not allowed to tote them. He emptied the chambers and said, "Hola."

They hesitated, then accepted the rifles. Now they looked askance at each other and at Sam. They walked very swiftly, on bowed legs. They wore the leggins and moccasins of their ilk. They were tougher than boots, Sam thought. If he took his eyes from them for a split second they would be gone like wild things.

Oddly, they had not far to go. There was a clearing on a hillside—Apaches could cling to rocks. Maybe twenty of them came to their feet as Sam rode in with his rifle still leveled. A middle-aged man squinted and said in Mexican Apache, "Is that you, Sam Jones?"

"Heard you were around, Aragon," said Sam. "These boys of yours are gettin' out of hand." He did not put his revolver in his belt. "You want trouble with me?"

"We want food."

"So shoot all the food you want. But if you come at me you know what happens."

"We have learned. I did not know it was you, Señor Sam. You have been a friend in the past."

"Those were the days." There had been an Indian girl, far from beautiful but good enough in a parched time. Both he and Aragon had been much younger.

"They see you now. They will know." Aragon was not conceding anything; he was stating fact.

Sam said, "There are people atop the mesa yonder." He gestured. "They must have a farm. They eat."

"There is a farm. Many guns."

"But you can raid it."

"It has been much danger. For a chicken."

Sam said, "If I give you bullets?"

Aragon said, "We will not shoot them at you or yours."

"Then you know who they are, on the mesa?"

Sam had guessed right. Aragon's gaze flickered. "Not good men."

"They will come down to Sunrise."

Aragon shrugged. "White man's troubles are not our troubles, Señor Sam."

"I am not asking for help. I'm telling you to stay clear. Here are bullets."

He reached into his saddlebag and took out a box of .44 shells. Now Aragon's eyes altered; his face worked for a moment. He accepted the gift. "We were very low. Muchas gracias."

"No gracias," said Sam in English. "Just work that farm; keep those bastids busy if you can. I'm sorry about the two younguns. They tried to kill us."

Aragon responded in his language, "Thus goes life. We are the people. We know how to leave this life."

"Adiós." It was time to leave when the pride began to rise, when they all moved uneasily. Sam wheeled the dun and rode away. They would not shoot him in the back, he knew, not after the gift of ammunition. They had their own code and it was better than that of a lot of whites he could mention. He rode back toward Sunrise. He had, he felt, accomplished little. He had, however, put himself in motion, corroborated his knowledge that Pitman had robbed the bank, and in a way he had made some amends for the deaths of the two Apache youths.

It was noon and Miss Terwilliger, the old-maid cashier, had gone to lunch. Adam was working as teller for the first time. Abe Solomon was watching, a benign smile on his face. Sally McLaine came waltzing in with a handful of bills and a small stack of coins. She went to the window and stared.

"Adam Burr! What are you doin' here?"

"At work," he said, grinning.

"You're a banker!"

"I'm a clerk. You like the idea?"

She was dubious. "I don't know. I never met a bank clerk. Leastways not that I know of."

He counted her money, and entered it in a book and on a piece of paper, which he filed. She watched with great interest as he gave her a receipt, scowling.

She said, "You sure have fancy handwritin', now, don't you, Mr. Burr?"

"Fancy doesn't count. Accuracy counts."

"My goodness! I don't suppose a banker would want to be seen with a dance hall gal." She tilted her nose.

"Why not?"

"It ain't—it ain't proper. Good afternoon, Mister Burr."

She stalked out with as much dignity as she could manage, her skirt swiveling with her hips. Sol came close to Adam and whispered, "Pay her no never mind. Already Missy Wagner is casting lamb's eyes at you."

Adam said, "That's sheep eyes, sir. All I want is to learn about banking."

"Ah, youth. Remember, Mayor Wagner is a wealthy man. Missy is a very proper young lady. Think, Adam, think of the future."

"Yes, sir. I certainly will." Missy Wagner was a very clever girl who could handle any part of the business of the bank, he had quickly learned. She was tall and thin and rather pretty, with large, violet eyes. She also had a quick tongue. He could not refrain from glancing at her as she sat over a new ledger in the corner. Their eyes met. She quickly looked down, her cheeks reddening.

Miss Terwilliger returned and Sol said, "Now, you two, go and eat and be back, no?"

Willy-nilly Adam left for the restaurant with Missy Wagner in tow. Passing the general store, he saw Sally McLaine at the dry goods counter. Further, she saw him, threw back her head, and turned away. Banking, he thought, was already becoming a difficult enterprise.

Missy Wagner said, "I understand you attended the College of Princeton in New Jersey, Mr. Burr. A fine institution. What did you learn in particular?"

"Nothing, really," he said absently, thinking of Sally McLaine. "I was not a very good student."

"Indeed." A few steps later she said, "I don't suppose you are aware that there is a social life in Sunrise beyond the El Sol Saloon. El Sol! The El Sol means 'the El Sol!' "

"Well, no one asked me to lead a cotillion as yet." She was getting on his nerves. " 'The El Sol' is common usage and okay."

"There will be a cotillion if those awful outlaws go away. Your friend Cemetery Jones has put a damper on all activities. People are too frightened to think of anything but danger."

"I've noticed," Adam said.

"I am no great admirer of Marshal Jones. He is a killer. Taking life means nothing to his sort."

"You believe that?"

They had come to Alec's Place, Cafe, Eatery. Adam said, "Should we have lunch and not berate my friend?"

"Or friends?" She sniffed and led him into the restaurant.

It was a difficult lunch, but he brought out all his Eastern manners and was, with some effort, polite. She represented, after all, a side of Western life he had not yet tasted. Live and learn, he thought, and all those other proverbs.

On the way back to the bank she took his arm and smiled and told him about the sewing circle and the Sunday school and the Christian Endeavor Society that tried to help the underprivileged. He went back to work without having assimilated much of her chatter. He returned her smile as she went to her desk and plunged into the array of figures Abe Solomon had assigned to him. He could hardly wait to return to the warm, rough atmosphere of the El Sol. At closing hour he lingered until Missy Wagner had departed, and then he hastened to the saloon.

Sam Jones was in his usual spot at the far end of the bar. He asked, "How'd it go?"

Adam told him. He was not in good spirits. He concluded, "Mr. Solomon is fine. I think I can learn a lot. It's time I began to study—which I never did at Princeton. But Missy Wagner . . . ugh!"

"Right pretty gal, I always thought."

"Right smart tongue."

"Well, there's always Sally."

"There was."

Sally McLaine entered. She went past them, saying, "Hi, Sam," and ran directly up the stairs."

Sam said, "Oh-ho."

"You see?"

Before Sam could reply there was a bellow from the street. "You yellow-bellied pukin' bastid tenderfoot, come out and fight like a man."

Adam started for the door. Sam caught him by the elbow and turned him around. "Got a rule. Remember? No fightin' in the streets."

"Am I supposed to let that big stiff get away with calling me names?"

Sam walked to the door. There were a half dozen toughs from Rafferty's with Harp Grogan. Sam looked them over, one at a time. Then he addressed Grogan. "You can shut your big mouth and quit disturbin' the peace or you can go to the hoosegow."

Grogan yelled, "I can whup the two of you together with one hand."

Adam said, "Please let me at him!"

"Matter of rules," said Sam. He said to the assemblage, "Rules. Go about your business or I'll have you all in jail."

Donkey Donovan appeared across the street, his shotgun comfortably under his arm. The toughs looked at him, then at Sam's holstered gun, then at Grogan. They shook their heads and departed.

"Cowards," Grogan shouted. "Afraid o' me. I ain't carryin' no gun. I fight with my fists. The hell with you. Yella-bellies, I calls y'all." He walked stiffly behind his friends toward Rafferty's saloon.

Jabez Wall and Harrison Deal appeared from somewhere behind Donkey. Wall called, "Grogan, I warned you. As of now you are no longer employed by me. Understand?"

Grogan called back, "And to hell with you, too, you pulin' old fool."

The two men came across the street. Wall said, "The man is a drunken boor. Ignore him, sirs. Let me buy you a drink."

"No, thanks," said Sam.

"You can see I accept no responsibility for any action taken or words spoken by Grogan."

"Yup."

"I believe in law and order. A peaceful existence in an orderly town,"

"Yup.

"I'm sure Mr. Burr can take care of himself. You are correct. He should pay no attention to foolish brags."

Sam and Adam went back to their places at the bar. Wall and Deal followed but stopped short of joining them. Renee and Sally came down the stairs and went to the piano. Mayor Wagner and two of the council, Frank Nixon of the general store and Morgan King of the mines, came to sit at their usual table. Adam was burning within.

He said to Sam, "Convy."

"Yeah." Sam sighed.

"You said it all."

"Yup."

"It has to be settled. You said that."

91

"Hoped you wouldn't remember." Sam reached for his drink. Shaky folded his hands and listened. Adam was unable to keep his voice down.

"You're teaching me. This may not be gunplay, but it's the same thing. Grogan won't stop."

"Yup."

"I have to fight him."

"Not in the streets," Sam said.

"I've got to fight him."

Renee drew close. Everyone was listening. Adam was adamant. Sam attended to his drink. He had that familiar foreboding nagging at him. Some things could not be prevented . . . . dangerous matters.

Renee said, "A benefit, for the poor?"

"Donkey's baby needs to go to El Paso to see a regular doctor," said Adam. "A benefit's all right with me."

"Grogan's a professional prizefighter," Sam told him.

"I won the intercollegiate," said Adam. "I'm not unskilled."

Jabez Wall said sonorously, "I will personally put up fifty dollars."

"Me too," said Harrison Deal. "We could stage it out of town limits and not break the law of Marshal Jones."

Now the mayor and the councilmen drew close. "Hey, it could quiet down the town. Give 'em something to think about exceptin' those damn—scuse me, ladies—outlaws."

Sam was thinking about the outlaws. "You reckon?"

"We'll put guards around so they can't make a rush," said Wagner. "Rifles on rooftops and all."

"Supposin' Adam whups him?" asked Sam. "He'd still be on the prowl, howlin' like a wolf."

Deal said, "Let it be known that the loser leaves town."

Adam gulped. Sam permitted himself a grin. Sally McLaine swallowed hard, then tried to appear indifferent. There was a long pause.

Adam said, "Let that be it."

"Abe Solomon ain't going to like this," said Sam.

"Don't you have confidence in me?" demanded Adam. "You think that big, drunken bum can beat me?"

Sam shrugged.

Shaky chimed in, "I'll put out four kegs of beer, proceeds to go to the poor."

"It'll be a town picnic," said Wagner.

"I'm for it," said Nixon. "I'll make a donation."

"I got a cleared lot north of town," said King. "Going to build a house on it. We could pitch the ring there."

A voice from the dim fastness of the far rear of the bar called, "This is a whale of a story!"

Shaky said, "That damn—scuse me, ladies—that damn Spot Freygang. Always hangin' around spyin'."

The photographer-reporter and part-time editor of the *Clarion Enterprise* came forward rubbing his hands, beaming. "Gimme a week. Just a week. I'll get out a special and have the whole country here. It'll be the biggest thing since the Fourth of July. We'll fill the town with people spendin' money. Just gimme a week to get some circulation."

For the first time Sam showed interest. "You reckon you can pull in a crowd like that?"

"What else is goin' on in these parts? You stopped the street fightin'; people are bitin' their nails over the outlaws. Been absolutely nothin' since you killed Convy. This is a big, big one!"

"I don't like it. I don't like it one bit," Sam muttered. But it would go on, he knew.

Mayor Wagner now said, "I got some experience as a referee, did you all know that? Yep. When I was a young feller. Worked some pretty good ones down on the border."

"There you go," said Jabez Wall. "Everything is falling into place. A fine thing for this town. Publicity and all. I'll take an ad, Freygang. Long John Mine, a few other enterprises in which I have an interest. When I bring the mill to

93

Sunrise we'll be more than a spot on the map, believe you me.''

"That's right," chimed in Harrison Deal. "A big affair!"

They're too anxious, thought Sam. Everybody's too anxious. "I still don't like it."

"The council. Let the council vote," said Mayor Wagner.

Sam looked at Adam with raised brows.

Adam said, "Like Convy. It's got to happen."

The council voted. There were three of them, unanimous. Spot Freygang ran for the newspaper office next to the undertaker. Sam returned to the end of the bar and ordered an unaccustomed double whiskey. Adam stood beside him.

Sam said, "Trainin'."

"I'm always in good physical condition," said Adam stiffly. "Grogan's a drunk."

"Early in the mornin'. You run."

"I have to be at the bank."

"Five o'clock," said Sam.

"Five o'clock!" Adam protested.

"I go with you."

"That's insane. Five o'clock."

Sally was standing at the piano. Renee played "Kathleen Mavourneen" and the girl sang. Adam reached for the whiskey bottle. Sam put it gently aside.

Adam said, "Aw, come on, Sam."

"The man's a professional. I seen pros fight."

"I can beat him anytime, anyplace."

"You sound like Grogan," said Sam. "Go to bed, damn early. Up at five." He turned away to listen more closely to the union of piano and voice. Inside him a dark cloud was forming.

As the top of the mesa Jabez Wall and Harrison Deal were out of breath from the climb. Pitman and the three Colemans—Frank, Jake, and Jesse—listened as they poured forth the story of the proposed fight between Grogan and Adam Burr.

Wall finished triumphantly, "Jones is bound to be in Burr's corner. Right out in the open."

"With guns all around and watchers everywhere," said Pitman. "Jones will be ready."

"But he'll be exposed. A target," said Deal.

"Sharpshooters in trees," added Wall. "Can't you manage that?"

Frank Coleman said, "It can be done, Rob."

"You think so?"

"We go down at night. There's a couple high trees. We lay up in there. A fast horse, that's it."

The two brothers chimed in, "We sure as hell can do it."

Pitman shook his head. "Not all of you. Maybe one of you."

"Hell, among us we can't miss," Frank Coleman boasted.

"And if they nail all three of you?"

After a moment Jake Coleman said, "I'm the best rifle shot."

"I got the fastest hoss," said Jesse.

"I'll do it," said Jake. "You gimme the time and I'll scout the place. This here is sure pop."

Pitman looked at the two city men. "What about Grogan?"

"Jones thinks we fired him. Maybe he can set Jones up. You know, grab him, spin him, something like that."

Deal was excited. "Don't you see? It's a perfect plan to get rid of Jones. Oh, perfect! If you only had your whole gang ready you could command the town under cover of the confusion."

"Why not?" demanded Wall. "You asked us for a plan. If Rafferty had some people ready it would work like a charm."

"If," said Pitman. He did not change expression. "And if the town wasn't more'n ready for just such a job."

Jake Coleman said, "I'll be there."

"He'll be there and he'll git Jones," said Frank. "You got to give us that chance."

"Yes. You get your chance. When Jones is dead we'll talk some more," Pitman said. The interview was ended.

"It will work," said Deal. "I've got this great feeling. It will work!"

The city men went back down the road from the mesa. When they were far out of earshot Wall said, "You damn fool."

"What do you mean?" Deal asked, offended.

"Rafferty and his men. I want them to be ready to defend the town. I want to get everything, you ninny. I want them to be ready and waiting when Pitman hits. I want them to get the loot. Then with Grogan we take it away from Pitman."

"From that man? You're the one who's crazy."

"You think so? Rafferty knows a few gunmen. Grogan handled a pistol in New York. All we need do is pretend Pitman got away. Bury him deep and keep the money. Return as saviors—but unluckily without the plunder."

Deal rode a while in silence. Then he said, "You do make big plans, Jabez. That you do."

"Big? Ah, Sunrise is nothin'. A headquarters off the beaten path. I'll own Sunrise, then we'll really make big plans. That fool governor in Santa Fe . . . Pah!"

"You dream, Jabez."

"How much cash do we have at our disposal?"

"I say . . . you dream. We have very little cash, Jabez."

"We must raise enough to satisfy the people of Sunrise."

"You have nothing left to mortgage but the Long John Mine," Deal said.

"Ah. Yes." Wall debated. "But that must be done in secret. After this fight with Grogan. You will go to Denver, El

Paso, wherever. Thus we will be ready, when we've disposed of Pitman, completed the scheme.''

"I can do that."

"Of course you can. I need your legal mind, friend."

"And I your imagination."

This agreed, they proceeded to town.

8

It was a strange week, a week of preparation, of hope, of confusion. Adam ran. Sam rode the dun horse alongside to make certain that he did. Abe Solomon was displeased. Renee talked among the citizens, urging them to contribute to the cause. Donkey Donovan was tearful in gratitude, especially when Sam advanced the money to send his wife and baby to the doctors in El Paso.

Missy Wagner scolded Abe Solomon. "It is a worthy cause. I think it is noble of Adam to risk himself against that big bully to help others."

"Pish tosh. Fisticuffs, pah! Nothing was ever solved by such nonsense."

"David slew Goliath!"

"And what did it get the Jews? Generations of persecution and a dead giant." Sol was not a believer.

Sally McLaine kept her own counsel. She deigned to nod to Adam, even to reply to his salutations. Otherwise she seemed strictly disinterested.

Harp Grogan stopped drinking. The crew at Rafferty's forced sobriety upon him when they discovered that Adam was training. Grogan scoffed but he gave in to popular demand.

Wall and Deal went around town seeking worthy causes that would benefit by the expected collection from the spectators of the event. There seemed to be a lessening of worriment among the citizens as the fight captured their imagination.

Adam lost weight, gained muscle and speed, and became short-tempered, especially with Sam riding the dun horse and urging him on—and on—and on. He missed his liquor and his pleasant evenings in the El Sol—and he missed Sally. He said to Sam, "Hell, I should just have met him on the street and knocked his block off."

"Against the rules," said Sam calmly. "Try to keep your left hand a little higher. You're a sucker for an overhand right."

"You know so damned much."

"I'm the marshal. I'm supposed to be smart." Sam could be, upon occasion, aggravatingly smug.

He was, however, far from smug about the coming event. He spent hours climbing onto roofs, up the high trees abounding in the town. He selected strategic points at ground level. He belabored the councilmen, demanding that each position he selected be occupied by an armed man, whether or not he had a view of the fight. It came down to drawing lots, so loath was everyone not to have a ringside spot.

The fight would be Sunday, all agreed, after church and during Sunday school so that the children would not be exposed to brutality. Not that a band of boys did not have plans of their own, of course. The church people would provide tea and cakes as opposed to Shaky's beer. All factions were in agreement that it was indeed a noble cause.

Friday evening in the El Sol Adam attempted to have words with Sally. She shrugged him off and made reference to his new profession, banker-boxer, and his new "interest" in "that skinny wench, the mayor's ugly daughter."

Saturday morning Missy Wagner invited Adam to dinner

at noon, steak and potatoes, the diet of a fighting man. Miffed at Sally's attitude, keyed up by the exertion of the training, he accepted.

Sally said to Sam, "You know he's now eatin' with those people?"

"You mean the Wagners? What you got against them?"

She glared. "Bankin'. Hangin' around with that hussy."

"You callin' Missy a hussy?"

Sally shook a fist. "She's right onto him all the time. She's after him, believe you me."

"Well, you don't care. You won't give him the time o' day."

"You're damn well right. I'm glad to be rid of the pulin' tenderfoot." She stomped upstairs to confide in Renee.

Shaky said, "Women. She won't go upstairs for no money. And she won't talk to the man who stopped her from so doin'."

"You ever been married?" asked Sam.

"Nope."

Sam paid attention to his drink. Too many ideas were coursing through his head. It was as sure as sunrise that something was brewing, that Pitman could not afford to overlook the opportunity to take action of some sort during the gala affair of the morrow. On the other hand, he was aware that Pitman knew the town would not be caught sleeping. It was a puzzlement.

Shaky was saying, "How did Sally know he was eatin' with the Wagners?"

"In a town this size everybody knows everything they want to know." That was it. Pitman would know everything he needed to know, because it was unquestionably true that there were people in town, notably the gang around Rafferty's, who would make reports. Further, there were Wall and Deal.

* * *

As the afternoon waned the El Sol filled up with men wagering. They bet on the winner; they bet on the round in which it would end; they bet on a knockout in rounds of choice. Some of the Rafferty crowd came in with money collected to bet on Grogan and were quickly covered. Spirits ran high, too high for Sam. He went out to patrol with Donkey, to make sure all the points of defense against surprise were safe and secure.

He went back to the El Sol and Renee had come downstairs. He spoke to her at the piano, where she was playing a soft but swinging lullaby. She said, "That girl upstairs is madly in love with Adam."

"She won't talk to him."

"You'll never understand why, my dear. You are not a woman, thank goodness."

"I'm a plumb worried old man," Sam said.

"Old?"

"I feel a million years old today. Tomorrow it'll be two million."

"You've covered everything," she assured him. "There can be no concerted attempt on the town."

"Nothin' is ever covered, not against Pitman and the Colemans."

"You are certainly correct. But then we could drop dead any minute, any of us, couldn't we?"

"Who wants to think like that?"

"No one. But take it easy, Sam. You've done your best."

"If Adam gets bad hurt or anybody gets killed, my best don't count."

She played a lively dance tune. Sally came down and whirled around with a customer.

Renee said, "The world is always with us, darling. If there's a tale to tell tomorrow—there'll be another day and time."

Sam had no answer. He looked at her long and hard. They

were not in the habit of touching in public, but their exchange was solid, profound. If his spirits were not restored, they were at peace when he left the saloon.

Atop the mesa Sandstorm and Montana rode up the path. Montana's left arm hung useless at his side, and Sandstorm had lost his sombrero. Pitman stared at them.

"Where's the vittles?"

"You ain't goin' to believe this," said Sandstorm, his eyes wild, his long hair disheveled. "We were plumb lucky to get away with our scalps."

"What the hell do you mean?"

"I mean a whole damn band of Apaches have took over the ranch. Scared them Mexicans of yours outa the country. The fodder's gone, the horses, everything. Some damn redskin yelled, 'Tell Señor Jones we are here.' "

"Jones?" Pitman's neck became red. "He sent Apaches to take over my ranch?"

"Farm," said Sandstorm. " 'Twas only a farm. No riders to make a fight, was there? Just farmers."

Pitman swallowed. "Yes. You're right. Absolom, how much we got left to eat?"

"Not near enough." The black man was attending to Montana's shoulder. "Hardtack. A few eggs."

Frank Coleman said, "Better let all three of us go down and clean up. You come behind us and make the raid when we git Jones."

"And get shot to pieces for our trouble," said Pitman. "No. Do what we planned. If we have to tighten our belts it won't be for long."

"How long?" Frank asked.

"Just until I make up my mind which way to go in. When Rafferty is ready."

"Rafferty. And how about those two gazabos who want part of the loot?"

"Let me worry about them," Pitman said.

"And about Rafferty?"

"Just keep your powder dry like they used to tell us in the war." Pitman had recovered his aplomb. "And make sure, damn sure, you get Jones tomorrow."

"We'll get him. We're talkin' on it," Frank told him.

They were robbers, thought Pitman, and until they had met Jones they had survived. They had outfoxed and outrun a dozen posses. They had killed aplenty, and they wanted Jones with every ounce of their bodies and souls.

But there were Harp Grogan and Wall and Deal to handle the town end, with Rafferty's help. Pitman thought he had Rafferty in his hip pocket, but then so did Wall and Deal. What had seemed a huge and profitable venture with little risk had become complicated. He held deep counsel with himself.

Donkey Donovan walked down the alleys, around the buildings on Main Street, cradling his shotgun and worrying about his wife and baby in El Paso. He came upon Sally McLaine in front of the hotel.

"Early for you, ain't it?" He touched his hat brim.

"Got a headache."

"Women have a lot of headaches," he said with sympathy. "You takin' that Lydia Pinkham medicine?"

"Whiskey's better. Can't take much of that, though." She lingered. "I'm glad your wife and kid got to go to El Paso. They say the doc down there sure knows about babies."

"They say." Donkey shook his head. "Sayin' ain't doin'. What I am is thankful for the help."

"No more'n people should do for people."

Donkey said, "You're goin' to the fight tomorrow, huh?"

"Oh, sure. She tried to make it sound offhand. "Who do you think'll win?"

"Well, if it ain't Adam I'm out a month's pay, which I shouldn't be bettin' by rights. But Grogan's a professional. Reckon it'll be a long, tough go."

"Adam Burr'll get that handsome face of his mussed up."

Donkey said, "Lordy, I seen fighters with their noses twisted almost to their ears. And ears like cauliflowers. Adam shouldn't have insisted."

"He's a damn fool."

"I wouldn't say that. Prideful, maybe too prideful." He squinted at her by the light reflected from the hotel lobby. "Some folks got altogether too much pride."

Sally said, "Donkey Donovan, you're as bad as the rest. Good night."

She flounced into the hotel. Donkey grinned to himself and continued his rounds. There were a few people still out on the streets, and the talk was almost entirely about the big event of the morrow. For the hundredth time he checked his position on the roof of the hotel, the highest spot in Sunrise. He would see little of the action in the ring, but he would have the most responsibility regarding the safety of the participants—and for that matter of the whole town. That was correct, he felt. He had been born here; his parents had been pioneers. He still felt guilt about the death of Dick Land; he still wanted to make up somehow for the loss of his mentor. He felt deepest gratitude toward Sam Jones, who had kept him on, had encouraged him in every possible fashion.

If he had a fault it was shyness. There had been no other kids to play with in his growing-up days, and his parents had been strong, quiet people. He had not yet been able to thank Sam in the proper manner. He vowed to remedy that omission tomorrow after the fight.

He walked. He saw Jabez Wall and Harrison Deal come from the direction of Rafferty's. It seemed odd that these businessmen should patronize Rafferty's, but then there was Grogan, who had worked for them. They were probably betting on him even though they had fired him. Donkey had a dim view of strangers who did not seem to fit into the life of Sunrise, the only life he knew. The pair went up to the hotel, but after a moment only Wall entered. Deal seemed to want a presleep stroll.

Sam Jones appeared at Donkey's side as though out of a silent sky. He, too, was looking toward the hotel. He said, "You see them come from Rafferty's?"

"Hi, Sam, you like to scare me to fits. No, just saw 'em comin' from that way."

"Me, too. Peculiar pair, them two."

"Just what I was thinkin'. People are stirrin' tonight."

"Go to bed, Donkey."

"Who, me? No time for bed yet."

"Want you sharp tomorrow. Clean that rifle," Sam said.

"I'll be ready."

"I know. Still, go to bed. I'm takin' over."

"Well, if you say so." Donkey gulped and went on, "Anything you say anytime, Sam."

"Okay, now." Sam patted his shoulder, a rare gesture on his part. "Sleep tight."

Donkey went obediently toward his home on the outskirts. Sam walked slowly, keeping in the shadows. Rafferty's was going strong. He stood in the batwing doors a moment without speaking. The sound diminished.

Rafferty said, "Ain't nothin' wrong goin' on here, Marshal. What the hell? Can't nobody have a li'l fun?"

"Keep it down." Sam vanished.

Rafferty said loudly, "Take it easy, boys. He won't be around here forever."

"Long enough," someone complained. "Mebbe too damn long."

Harp Grogan, sipping sarsaparilla, growled, "You listen to Rafferty. Wait'll tomorrow."

"You ain't fightin' Sam Jones," another called out.

"I can lick him and his tenderfoot together, one hand," said Grogan. "You wait."

Rafferty said, "So long as us people hang together we got a chance to be rid of the marshal. So shut up and have a drink on the house."

It was a plea never denied. They drank and were not so noisy as before.

Adam awoke in a cold sweat. He had been dreaming of his boyhood, the vague figure of his father, his domineering mother. He pulled on pants and shirt and picked up his rifle. He went out the back door of the bank, locking it with care. He walked up the alley to Main Street. He almost ran into the figure of Harrison Deal.

"Ah, nervous, no doubt?" The man was pleasant enough. "I understand, my boy. I understand."

"Just getting a breath of fresh air." Adam walked the width of the bank building, turned to retrace his steps. Deal stayed beside him.

"You'll beat Grogan," he said. "You have youth and strength. People like you are the future of the West."

"Thank you," said Adam, wishing the lawyer would go away, thinking not of the fight but of Sally McLaine.

"May I ask a personal question?" Deal asked.

"You may ask. I may answer."

"Was your father named Alexander Burr?"

"Whose ship your friend Mr. Wall salvaged?" Adam was cool, every sense alert at once.

"This is correct. Your poor father was missing when Jabez boarded with intent to give aid."

"So I heard."

"Well . . . so it was. We wish you well tomorrow. Our mistake in associating with Grogan will be somewhat ameliorated if you win," said Deal. He bowed and turned back toward the hotel.

The man leaked oil, Adam thought. Insincerity poured from him. As Sam had surmised and often said, there was something very fishy about the two, Wall and Deal.

Adam saw Sam approaching and was immediately defensive, heading toward the rear of the bank.

Sam watched him unlock the door, made no attempt to speak or follow him inside. Adam paused, shifting the rifle from one hand to the other. "I wasn't out of sight or sound for a minute," he said.

"Yup. I noted. What did the lawyer have to say?"

"He asked about my father. Said he was gone when they went aboard the ship."

"You didn't believe him."

"How would I know? The man's too slick. I know that."

"Slicker than Wall. But not as crafty," Sam said. "You got the heaves tonight?"

"The heaves? Oh, like a horse. No. Just woke up and needed air."

"You'll sleep," said Sam. "You got until noon."

"I'll sleep." Adam felt defiant.

"Looks like everybody's a bit tetchy. Sally went home early. Told Donkey she had a headache. Happened to over hear."

"What do I care about Sally?"

"Just thought I'd mention it. Reckon Missy Wagner's havin' a troublesome night, too."

"You're making fun of me, Sam. Good night!" Adam went inside and slammed the door. He didn't hear Sam's chuckle. He was so annoyed he fell asleep at once.

Frank and Jake Coleman rode through the darkness. When they came to the tall tree they stopped. Frank said,

"You're the best climber, too. Too bad you got to spend all that time up there, though."

Jake said, "We slept in trees before."

"Well, this time we get somethin' for it. The bastid. I can see poor Tim now, dead as a doornail."

Jake said, "We goin' to make damn sure. Brother, I want you to take my horse back with you."

"That's loco!"

"You think so? You think that damn Cemetery Jones won't be prowlin'? He sees that horse, I'm a dead man."

"If you ain't got a ride tomorrow you're just as dead," Frank said.

"No. I shoot Jones, everybody scatters. Afore they can get together I'll be back in camp afoot."

"You reckon?"

Jake said, "Look, we done swore to get Jones. He killed our brother. If he lives, our name'll be a joke. People will always remember. Cemetery Jones killed a Coleman and got away with it. That don't go down. I'll get him, and there ain't nobody in that town can get me, horseback or afoot. You can believe that, brother."

Jake had been next youngest to Tim. He was the quiet Coleman and now there was in him deep fanaticism. It was he who had kept the impetuous youngest brothers under control until the fatal day they essayed to ambush Cemetery Jones. There was no denying him.

Frank said, "Rob ain't goin' to like it."

"You tell Rob Pitman he ain't bossin' the Colemans. You're the boss of us. You can wait and let me tell him after I git Jones."

Frank said, "I got to say I don't like it, Jake."

"Always I listened to you. It ain't I don't respect you. Nohow. It's just I got to do this."

"I can see it." Frank watched Jake sling his rifle over his shoulder, clamber up onto the saddle, and take hold of the lowest branch of the giant tree. He whispered, ''So long, Jake. So long.'' He waited until his brother was out of sight, then rode back to the mesa, leading Jake's horse.

When Donkey Donovan tapped on Sam Jones's door it was early morning. The town was already astir, the church bell was pealing, and Sam was bathed and dressed in jeans, soft boots, a light blue wool shirt—and his gunbelt. The sun had just topped the eastern mountains and was playing kaleidoscope games with the pyrite on the slopes to the west.

Sam said, "Good mornin'. Had your coffee?"

"Alec wasn't open. Didn't sleep much." Donkey presented his Winchester. "You want to check?"

"No way. You're the man with the gun. Coffee."

They went down and greeted people as they walked Main Street. The fight was to be at noon, when the sun would not interfere with either man. Adam Burr came toward them. He was dressed in light eastern trousers, low walking shoes, and a linen shirt. He was bronzed and his eyes were clear and so far as Sam could see, he was not in the least nervous.

Adam said, "Hi. Coffee?"

"Eggs and ham and pancakes and milk for you," said Sam.

"I suppose so. Not hungry, not really. Just an empty feeling." He grinned at them. "I'd like to fight him right here and now."

"You don't get your druthers," said Sam. They went into the restaurant.

Spot Freygang was waiting, his heavy camera equipment nestling in a corner. He leaped to greet them.

"Hi, gents. How do you feel, champ? Okay? Ready?"

Adam said, "Who wants to know?"

"The paper. We're gonna cover every minute of your day."

Sam said, "You're gonna leave him alone. And you be damn careful with that camera. If you blast off powder and blind my man, you will be the sorriest jasper in Sunrise."

Undisturbed, Freygang said, "I worked that out. I got a method. My own discovery. I shoot up. See? Up from layin' on the ground. I get 'em when they're facin' each other. No danger to their eyes."

"You better had." Sam led Adam to the far corner away from the reporter. Donkey stood guard even as he ate his breakfast, warding off casual invaders.

Adam said, "This is worse'n fighting. They mean well, but they get on a fellow's nerves."

"Eat slow and we'll get clear," said Sam. It was like a gun showdown, he knew. Concentration was a great part of it all. He drank coffee and was silent, turning away all questions, all attempts at encouragement. Sally McLaine came in with Renee and Sam scowled. He went at once to lead them to a table as far from Adam as could be managed.

"You gals are up early," he said, sitting down, placing his hat on an empty chair.

"Why not? The street is full of men with guns," said Renee. "Males with a case of the vapors."

"No vapors for you two."

"Maybe we're interested in the fight," said Renee. "Maybe we didn't sleep any better than you did."

"I slept."

"With one eye open," Renee said, smiling. She looked, as always, fresh and composed, attired for out-of-doors in a divided skirt and a blouse.

"Will he get bad hurt?" Sally spoke in a voice Sam had not heard before, subdued, almost a whisper.

"Oh, I don't reckon Adam will kill him," said Sam.

"Damn you." Sally returned her attention to ordering breakfast, soft boiled eggs and toast and coffee.

Renee said, "When men fight, they get hurt. It's a question of how bad."

Sam said, "Ladies, there is all kinds of hurt. Some are a lot worse'n others. Adam is doin' what he believes he has to do. He ain't worryin' too much about the fight." He looked hard at Sally, then picked up his hat. "If they're on the streets already I better get to movin'. See you later."

Adam had not finished his meal; he was toying with the remains and trying not to stare at Sally. Sam went to Alec, a man with a hound-dog face and the disposition of a scared rabbit, and gave him a bill. "That's for Renee, Sally, Adam, Donkey, and me. Keep the change."

Alec said, "Good luck, Marshal. I wouldn't be either of those hombres for a million of them bills."

"No danger," said Sam.

He took Adam by the shoulder and marched him out-of-doors. The sun was creeping higher; it would be a hot day. Sam said, "Up to my room. Lock the door. Don't move any more'n you have to. Sleep if you can. I'll be checkin'."

"I can't do that."

"You'll do it because I tell you." Sam's voice became crisp, authoritative. "You come this far. You go the rest of the way."

"Too damn much fuss and feathers."

"Yup." Sam marched him to the hotel, shoved him upstairs, into the room. He locked the door, took a deep breath, and went down to attend to his job as policeman, a task he particularly disliked on this day. There he was, listening again to that small voice inside him, too much at stake for a Sunday. He wondered if all those people in church were praying for Adam and if it would be any help.

He made his way to the site of the ring, which was constructed under the London Prize Ring Rules as dictated by Mayor Wagner. Men were busy digging holes for eight posts, around which would be strung three strands of rope. The opponents would toe a mark at ring center. Wagner was intoning, "The use of rasslin' holds are allowed. When a man is down his seconds may drag him to his corner and work on him for thirty seconds; then the fight begins again from scratch. There ain't no kickin' nor gougin' allowed, nor hittin' a man when he is down or even on one knee. It's all writ down and I got the book."

Sam said, "You got it. Has Grogan got it?"

"Grogan knows it," said Wagner. "He also knows I got it and that he can be disqualified if I say so."

"That's good enough for me." The grass had been trimmed and rolled the previous day and all seemed in order. Self-important teenagers stood guard, chasing away smaller kids, helping the laborers as best they could.

The mayor said, "Got me out of goin' to church any old how. Best we meet the council at the El Sol."

A half dozen horsemen kicked up dust entering Main Street, led by Tex Tillus and Abe Porter. They hallooed, tied up, and went into the saloon.

Sam said, "You ain't goin' to need me. Nixon and Morgan'll be there. Work things out like we planned."

"Just like you say. How's Adam?" the mayor asked.

"Sleepin'." At least Sam hoped so.

"He's a good boy."

"Yup."

"My Missy's plumb fond of him."

"Most people are." Sam made his way to the bank. He went around and tapped on the back door. Sol opened it and peered at him.

"Foolishment. I'm ashamed of you, Sam."

"Yup." Sam entered the office where Adam had slept

during the week of training. It had a musty smell. Sol looked old and worn. "You worry too much."

"Who will worry if not me? I'm the keeper of the money. The root of all evil."

"There'll be others protectin' the evil," Sam told him.

"And who will protect the boy?"

"His own strong arms."

"And Jehovah?"

"There's the people will be prayin' in church."

"Yech! Because they have money bet on him. Never mind his nose," Sol said.

"It's up to him to protect his nose. He'll be all right. He's a new man in town. From now on he'll be a native, win, lose, or draw."

Sol spread his hands. "Of course you are right, my friend. Make money or make brave and the West is yours."

"And you love it here."

"I accept that which I cannot prevent."

"The boy could marry Missy Wagner and work for you and settle down and be a citizen. It just ain't his way."

"He's a fine worker in the bank. Smart, quick."

Sam said, "He has to follow his marks. For all of us there's marks to follow if we see them."

Sol's spirit lightened. "Sam, Sam. You are a man of vision. Why else did I come here, to this glorious western country? Like you said. So go and do."

"Yup." Sam left. The old man was himself a fine example of what the country was becoming; therefore, he could see the light. It was enough for now.

Sam walked among people bustling on this strange Sunday. They were singing in the church. Renee would be playing the wheezing old organ. He wondered if Sally had accompanied Renee—probably the first time the girl had ever been within the hallowed precincts.

He came to the smithy. Holcomb was lounging, smoking a smelly pipe. Sam asked, "You got it in shape?"

CEMETERY JONES

"I can wheel it and my sons can run it and I can shoot it."

The cannon had been polished, a sturdy, dangerous instrument. The two Holcomb boys were in their teens, one powerful like his father, the other a slender, redheaded lad. They grinned at Sam and showed him how they could maneuver the little fieldpiece.

"You can bring it to the fight," Sam promised.

"Not no way," said their father. "There's work to do and we're away behind. But we'll be on call."

The boys lifted their shoulders in resignation. Neither seemed resentful. They were, Sam thought, a lot better behaved than he had ever been.

He walked down to the church. In the yard was an arsenal of weapons of all sizes and calibers, carefully stacked. No outlaw with a grain of sense would make an attack on a town so ready, he thought. Rob Pitman had plenty of savvy. Even the Colemans would not be that stupid, lusting as they must be for his life's blood.

He proceeded toward Rafferty's. The little warnings deep in his gut were mumbling indistinct advice. Truthfully, he did not approve of this pseudo prizefight perched precariously on the notion of charity. It smacked of hypocrisy, he thought, well-meaning but hollow. Even Renee had been carried away with the idea, along with the churchly and the riffraff—and the city council. Only Adam, anxious as he was to get at Grogan, had expressed doubts as to the means thereof.

There were too many horses tied up at Rafferty's Saloon. Sam checked one with the Bar X brand. It had been altered so badly that he knew it to be stolen from the P I over in Arizona where he had once been foreman for a spell. A cursory examination told him there was a band of horse thieves in town.

He entered. A tall man with a long nose slanted grotesquely toward his left ear said, "Hi, Sam. How's it goin'?" He rubbed his nose. "Ain't seen you in a long time. Not since you gimme this."

Sam said, "Too short a time, Shanks."

"Came over to see the fun. Me and some friends."

"Fun."

"You know. The fight."

Sam said, "Yup. You heard about the rule?"

Shanks lifted long arms. "Search me. No weapons."

"I don't search folks," said Sam.

Shanks turned to the crowded room. "Truth, he tells. Real truth. He shoots first, searches later. Any of you don't know about Cemetery Jones, ask me. I'm expert."

"Tell 'em about sundown, Shanks."

"Aw, we all know that. We'll be gone long afore sundown." A crooked grin went with the crooked nose. "Nobody's buckin' this town, Sam."

Rafferty said, complaining, "You don't make that speech in the El Sol, Marshal. Tell them hymn-singin' people to behave too, and we'll all git along better."

Sam stared at him. Then he shook his head in resignation, turned on his heel, and walked out. The air was better in the street. Church was letting out and people were talking and waving their arms and acting as though the circus had come to town. He did not like it one bit. He looked at his watch. It was eleven-thirty, time to arouse Adam. Shaky was closing the doors of the El Sol. Mayor Wagner and the council met him at the hotel.

Sam said, "Just talked to the sneakiest horse thief in six territories. Put some men on the stable and make sure everything's nailed down tight."

"You talkin' about Shanks Totten?" demanded Tillus, the rancher. "For Gossake. I'll put my men on him."

"You do that."

The councilmen started for the scene of the fight. Missy Wagner tripped around a corner and ran up to Sam. "Is

Adam all right?'' she asked breathlessly. ''I had to run home and change from my Sunday clothes.''

''You look right fine,'' Sam assured her. ''I'll take best care of Adam that I can.''

''He's so polite. You should see him at dinner, such manners and all.''

''I've seen him eat. Very nice.''

''Marshal.'' She moved close and lowered her voice. ''Do you think there's anything serious betwixt him and that . . . that saloon girl?''

''Now, why should you ask me a question like that?'' Sam became round-eyed, innocent. ''I'm the peace officer, not the society editor. Why'n't you ask Spot Freygang? He knows all that goes on in town.''

She backed off, tossing her head. ''I'll do my own thinking on it. Thank you just the same.''

She went toward the fight ring, walking stiffly as a real lady should. Sam sighed and went into the hotel.

The clerk's wife, still wearing her church bonnet, looked at him disapprovingly. ''John's gone off with the other sinners. Deputy Donovan's on the roof. Mr. Burr is making noises in your room.''

''Thank you, ma'am.'' Sam went up to the stepladder leading to the roof. Donkey was looking through field glasses, sweeping the countryside. ''People look like a pack of ants,'' he said. ''Can't see nothin' out of the ordinary, Sam.''

''There's a gang at Rafferty's. Rustlers. Maybe they just came for the fight. Maybe not.'' He described Shanks Totten.

''I seen them come in. Tillus's riders been sorta hangin' around in sight of Rafferty's.''

''Good. Don't let that glass keep you too close on the fight.''

''It's a temptation,'' admitted Donkey. ''But I know why I'm up here, Sam, believe me.''

"Sure you do."

Sam went back down the ladder. Adam admitted him to the room, naked from the waist up, sweating. He was also grinning. "Slept good, Sam. I'm warmed up nicely."

"Right. We better go."

Adam sobered. "Sam, that lawyer, Deal. Why did he go out of his way to tell me about Father?"

"He could be lyin'," said Sam. "On t'other hand he could be scared. Might think you'd take him on next."

"That's foolishment."

"Yup. Just don't want you thinkin' about anything but the next hour or so."

"Oh. I see. Okay, let's go," Adam said.

The streets were now empty except for horses tied to railings and switching their tails against the flies. The sun was at its apex and Sunrise at noon was as bare of shadow as on the blackest of nights. Adam wore a long robe over tight, lightweight trousers. His feet were in moccasins bought for the purpose by Mayor Wagner, who was thoroughly in charge of the scene, it quickly developed. The townspeople stood by—on the sward, on boxes, crates, benches—anything to give them a point of vantage.

Ringside was reserved for the council—and three ladies. People stared, but Renee, Sally, and Missy Wagner held their positions near the corner designated for Adam. Missy held her head high until she was joined by a jittery Miss Terwilliger from the bank, when she began to whisper in that lady's ear and nod her head with great vigor.

When Sam led Adam to his corner, the roar of the crowd stirred the birds in the adjoining trees so that they set up a great croaking in protest. By unspoken mutual agreement, one side of the terrain was held by the mob from Rafferty's, including the coterie brought in by Shanks Totten. Sam looked it all over with great care. Harp Grogan and Rafferty had not yet appeared.

"Tired old play," he told Adam. "Figures to make you nervish."

Adam was looking at Sally, who was not looking back at him. Sam glanced at Spot Freygang, who was at midring facing north, his unwieldy camera resting on a contraption that was set upon a swivel of some kind. The reporter waved a hand, grinning. Wall and Deal stood nearby. Freygang aimed the camera up at them and fired off powder, startling many of the spectators into brandishing their guns.

Order restored, Mayor Wagner walked across the squared circle and said, "Sam, you're allowed another second. You know, in case you have to carry Adam to the corner."

Adam said, "I won't need carrying."

"He can rassle you down, trip you," the mayor pointed out.

Sam was inspired. He called, "Mr. Deal."

The lawyer was taken aback. "Yes, Marshal?"

"Would you oblige us by helpin' me in the corner?"

Deal said, "Why . . . I hardly know . . . I mean, I've never done anything like that."

Sam said, "Neither have I."

Jabez Wall nudged his partner forward. "An excellent idea. You go ahead."

The lawyer came slowly. He removed his jacket and hung it on the ring post. He wore a somewhat soiled white shirt with sleeve garters. There was some applause, some laughter. The crowd was getting restless under the hot sun.

Sam said, "You just watch me and do like I say."

"Oh, I will. I will." Deal tried to smile.

Sam removed Adam's linen robe and threw it loosely over the young man's wide brown shoulders. "Just keep calm. Don't even look at Grogan when he shows."

"I won't." Adam returned his gaze to Sally.

On the roof of the hotel, Donkey moved slowly, the field glasses sweeping the countryside. Kids ran in and out among the people, shouting; parents tried to control them.

Sally looked everywhere but at Adam. Renee stood cool and aloof, a small smile playing at the corners of her mouth. Shaky stood guard over his kegs of beer up on the slope to the west. Two youths were dispensing the lukewarm suds. There was a coterie now of church ladies, sternly standing their ground apart from Sally and Renee, centered around a determined Missy Wagner, who chattered uncontrollably. Sally fixed her finally with an unwavering stare.

Sam said to Harrison Deal, "If anything goes wrong, you be ready one way or t'other."

"Wha-what do you mean, Marshal?" the lawyer asked.

"Just what I said."

"But . . . but . . ."

There was a roar from the Rafferty side. The saloon keeper and a brawny black man named Izaak were escorting Harp Grogan through a path made by shoving and hauling. They came to the ring and Spot Freygang again shot off his flash.

Grogan was naked to the waist, hairy, looking much bigger than when clothed. His arms bulged, his shoulders sloped; his belly was solid as an oak barrel. He posed, turning, manipulating his biceps. He glared at Adam and said something indistinguishable under his breath. Rafferty hustled him to his corner, where he stood straight, still staring. Mayor Wagner went to ring center and held up a hand for silence. Oddly, he got it.

"This here fight will be under the London Prize Ring Rules," he declaimed. "Both men know them. If either one breaks one of 'em he'll be disqualified and all bets will be paid accordingly."

Rafferty said, "We know the damn rules. Start the fight and let's get it over with."

"T' hell with all that. Lemme at him," roared Grogan.

Wagner said, "Toe the mark." He drew a mark in the short grass with the edge of his boot at ring center. The robe fell from Adam's shoulders, the sun gleaming on his tanned body, slim as compared to that of Grogan. They marched to the mark. Grogan put up his fists. Adam stood motionless, arms at his side.

Wagner drew his gun, lifted it, held a moment, then fired a shot into the air. The crowd exploded with the signal.

Grogan reached out to seize Adam, who was not there. He had sidestepped and ducked and now both his fists spat out, landing on Grogan's body, raising welts as the big man howled his rage.

Grogan rushed. Adam moved right, then left. He played a tattoo on Grogan's face. The big man wheeled, faster than it seemed possible for a man his size. He caught Adam by surprise, buried him in a bear hug. His strength was truly enormous. He bent a knee and laid Adam over it as though to break his back.

Adam relaxed, went limp. Then he rolled, jamming an elbow into Grogan's groin. He was falling even as he made his move and Wagner called in foghorn style, "Time!"

Sam was there in a flash, Harrison Deal uncertainly following. Adam coughed, regaining his breath as Sam led him to the corner.

"Kneel, man, kneel," said Sam.

Harrison Deal got down on one knee. Adam perched there at Sam's insistence.

"That'll be about it," Sam said. "Thirty seconds to get back your wind. Stay away from him if you can."

Adam said, "Ugh."

Morgan King was holding the watch. He said, "Time."

Adam slid from Deal's knee. He went forward. Grogan rushed again. Adam sidestepped again. Grogan whirled around, arms bent, seeking a hold, as in wrestling. Adam did a dance step, in and out, and dealt punishment—right, left, right, left—then switched style and went left, right, left, right. Each blow landed cleanly—and seemed to have no effect upon the raging bull of a man who still pursued him.

Now the daily running stood Adam in good stead. He moved like a bullfighter, darting out of the clutch of the giant at the last possible second, dealing rapid blows to his face and neck, avoiding the clinches with ease. Grogan stopped dead and threw a roundhouse right aimed at Adam's head that might have decapitated him.

Adam ducked, stepped inside for the second time, and rammed his fists at the big man's belt. He was hitting the most solid flesh, but there had to be a limit. His blows came from the hip, his weight behind them. Grogan's mouth opened; he gave ground.

Adam pursued. He brought an uppercut that landed on the giant's neck. Grogan gasped, spun around, took another punch, and measured his length upon the green.

"Time!"

Grogan came up instantly, slobbering, red-faced with rage. He started for Adam, who had stepped back.

Sam was between them. Grogan seized him and spun him with his back toward the north. Spot Freygang pointed his camera and let go with a huge flash of powder. Instantly there was gunfire.

Harrison Deal screamed. Donkey Donovan shouted something from the rooftop. There was a crashing of branches as a body hurtled down from the top of a tall tree.

Adam sprang forward. Grabbing Grogan by the shoulder, he broke him away from Sam. He leveled a right fist. It went straight to the mark, the base of the jaw. Grogan pitched forward and lay quite still.

Sam had his revolver in his hand. He said to Adam, "Get back and lay low."

Donkey was still firing into the tree. Adam, confused, looked to Harrison Deal. The man lay flat, his arms extended.

"Sam!" cried Adam. "Here!"

Sam came running. There was a hole in the lawyer's

chest. From afar, under the tall tree, one of Tillus's cowboys called, "Hey! We got a deader here."

Now the crowd milled. Adam felt someone near. He turned and Sally McLaine was throwing his robe about him, interposing her slight body between him and possible further gunfire. Her face was dead white. He put his arm around her and held her tight beneath the robe.

In all the confusion Mayor Wagner stood his ground. At the top of his lungs he shouted, "I declare Adam Burr the winner of this here fight."

There was none to say him nay. Grogan did not stir. Missy Wagner had fainted; the church ladies gathered around her. Renee made her way to Sam's side.

She said, "I caught a glimpse of it. I was turned away from the flash. A man in that tree fired."

"At me," said Sam.

"Quite probably. The flash must have blinded him." Behind her Freygang said excitedly, "What a story! Cameraman spoils murder."

"You better look at Mr. Deal," said Sam dryly. "Seems like you need different wordin'."

Renee said, "Then Donkey fired from the roof."

Tillus broke through the crowd. "It was Jake Coleman. You can bet it was a whizzer, Sam. That bastid Grogan—scuse me, Miss Renee—that bastid spun you with your back to Coleman. Jake musta waited all night for that chance."

"He'd wait a year." Sam felt sneaking admiration for the dead Coleman. "They want me that bad."

Jabez Wall was kneeling beside the lawyer. In his mind only one thought repeated itself over and over. That vault in Frisco. That vault where Deal told about the shipwreck and all. That vault will be opened. I can't cover this up; the newspaper's got it. That vault . . . I got to move. I got to move fast. That damned stinkin' lawyer's trick.

Adam was still holding on to Sally McLaine. As the crowd broke up they walked together beneath his robe to the hotel. Renee watched them, smiled, and went toward the El Sol.

Under the tall tree Doc Bader said, "He's as dead as he'll ever be. Nice shootin', Donkey."

"I seen him when the camera went off. Dumb luck, mebbe."

"The flash made him miss the marshal," said Freygang, setting off another to mark the incident for history. "I got to run and get Mr. Wall. His friend was always ready to give me a story." He said, "Hey, I'm a sorta hero, right?"

"You're a damn nuisance," said Sam Jones. "But this time, thanks."

Donkey said, "We all know he was gunnin' for you, Sam. Hadda be, him a Coleman."

"Yup," said Sam. He shrugged and walked down Main Street. For once it was quiet in Rafferty's. A lot of money had changed hands. They were still pouring whiskey over and into Harp Grogan, who was throwing it up as fast as it went in.

Sam turned in at the bank. Sol sat in his office, sober-faced, inquiring.

"So?"

"I never did like it," said Sam. "The town will go right back to where it was."

"Scared."

"Yup."

"There'll be talk against you, no?" Sol asked.

"And not only from Rafferty's," Sam agreed.

"First they beg you to take the badge. Now they'll say you drew fire, got a citizen killed. We know that."

"Yup."

"You have ideas?"

"Give Adam some leeway. Have them make him a deputy. He's to be trusted."

"Not with the ladies."

"Never mind that." Sam smiled slightly.

"Of course. Like you say."

"I'll be seein' you."

Sam went to the hotel. As he expected, Renee was waiting in his room.

She put her arms around him. "Thank God for Donkey Donovan."

"And the photographer."

"The mysterious ways of fate," she said. "The council is still quivering in the El Sol."

"Yup."

"Jabez Wall is wailing at the loss of his friend. He will, he said, have to leave town at once to take care of their affairs."

"I could bet on that."

"There's a connection between him and the attempt."

"No way to prove it." Sam shook his head.

"So you'll go out on your own."

"You know me real good."

"They'll be looking for you."

"They ain't fools."

"Rafferty's crowd will be working here," she told him.

"I won't be here."

"I see the logic. But oh, the danger."

"No worse'n today. I was a target today."

"Rather the hunter than the hunted."

He was quiet, sitting on the edge of his bed, staring at his hands. "Renee, I'm a killer. Oh, I know. I try to be on the right side. But when I think that anyone could've been shot down by that crazy fool in the tree I want to kill."

"Not necessarily a Coleman. Whoever is behind it."

"Ron Pitman, the other Colemans, any of them."

"That, my dear, is seeking justice, preventing further crime."

"Maybe," he said.

"You mean it could have gone the other way."

"Take Convy. I never gave him a chance. Go back to Tim Coleman. I might've winged him. It's in me, Renee."

She sat beside him, taking one of his hands in both of hers. Her voice was throaty, scarcely audible. "Believe me, Sam, I know. I've never told you and you've never asked. But there was a time when I found it in me. It lies somewhere in all of us. A time to kill."

They embraced, fiercely, more intensely than ever before. The tie that bound them grew tighter.

In Rafferty's secret back room Jabez Wall said, "I tell you it's got to happen now, at once. While the town is jittery."

"See Rob Pitman," Rafferty said.

"I mean to do that at once. Do you be ready."

"I brought in a hard bunch. My men are ready. They lost their shirts on Grogan; they're more'n ready."

Wall leaned closer, his eyes gleaming. "Jones and that Burr fellow. You understand?"

"Jones, sure. But the tenderfoot, no. He ain't nothin' to worry about."

"He's guarding the bank. He's close to Jones. You see?" Wall was pushing hard now. "When the fire starts they'll be in the open. They must be killed."

"If we can find 'em. But I still say you got to see Pitman."

"As I said. Right now."

"The boys got a horse for you. Out back." Rafferty gestured toward the door.

"I'm going. I will return. Be ready." Wall's mind was turning around like a mill wheel. If he could get the cash he might bribe someone in San Francisco. If he could put all his holdings together he might laugh at Deal's confession. Power, he needed power. For that he needed cash; the cash to flee, to take another name. South America. Anyplace. He was cornered, but he had time to get out of it, he thought.

News did not travel that fast. There would be some delay in closing that damned lawyer's estate. There was a way. There had to be a way.

10

The moon played tricks on the troubled town. Two bodies lay in Spade's funeral parlor. Sam Jones sat in his office by the light of a dim lamp. The shades were drawn against an attack by a passerby. Donkey Donovan entered behind two protesting drunks from Rafferty's and shepherded them to the cells.

Sam looked them over. They quieted down when he asked their names, their home places, their destination in the morning when, he assured them, they would be leaving on the stage. Death, he thought, had a way of penetrating even the drunken mind.

Back in the office he said to Donkey, "I'll be leaving soon."

"Like you planned."

"Do what you can to keep it peaceful. You know what else to do."

"I can do it. Today made me feel I can do what you want."

"Don't stay up too late."

"One more round." Donkey gulped. "I just hope my baby's gonna be all right."

"She'll be all right," Sam said kindly. "Good night."

Donkey departed. Mayor Wagner came in before the door could close.

"Gettin' late, but I wanted to talk to you, Sam," he said.

"It figures."

"I . . . God, my daughter was there. She fainted."

"Yup."

"That Burr boy, he's been triflin' with her affections."

"Has he now? For true?"

Wagner squirmed. "Well. He went off with Sally and we haven't seen him since."

"You got something against Sally?"

"Well. Hell, no. But Burr, he's a banker now, and it don't seem right."

"Seemin' ain't is."

"Okay. Okay. Well. The council's upset. Those Colemans are after you. Killed an innocent man. Who else? Might've killed any of us."

"Especially you, where you were when it happened," Sam pointed out.

"Right. Well, me or anybody else."

"Meanin' I'm a danger to the town."

"Damn it, Sam, without you we're up the creek. With you we got bushwhackers takin' shots at us."

Sam said, "That's right on both counts. Tell you what. You look to Donkey for a time."

"What do you mean?"

"Don't talk to anybody. If they ask about me, say you sent me on some errand. Anything."

"Where you goin'?" Now the mayor was alarmed.

"Best you don't know."

"You ain't quittin'?"

Sam smiled. "You ain't sure whether that'd be good or bad, are you, amigo?"

"Hell, Sam . . ."

"It don't matter. Like I said, what is . . . is. We've got to go with it. You run along and do the best you can."

"Well." The mayor was in a true quandary. "Okay, Sam." He departed, shoulders hunched.

Sam took his rifle from the glass case that had been installed to house official weaponry. He filled a belt with cartridges and strapped it around his shoulders. He was traveling light this time. He locked the office and went back to the hotel. He knocked on Adam's door.

"That you, Sam?" Adam called.

"Yup."

The door opened at once; Adam was wide awake. They sat down and Sam grinned and Adam flushed. The scent of Sally McLaine was still in the room.

Adam said, "You saw how she came running, trying to protect me from a bullet."

"Yup."

"Bank or no bank. I mean the hell with everything."

"Yup."

"I'm going to tell Abe Solomon how I feel."

"Wouldn't bother. It'll show, one way or the other," Sam said.

"She's a wonderful girl."

"Yup."

"What's into you? Why the extra cartridge belt?" Adam asked.

"Makin' another pasear."

"Alone?"

"It's like this, podner. It's goin' to happen. There's two dead today. Don't give a hoot about either of 'em. But it makes the town ready, scared ready. You savvy?"

"Uh—yes. It becomes inevitable because the town is inviting trouble."

"I want to know how and when. Rafferty brought in some boys, y'know. How does Rob Pitman see it? He's smart. The two survivin' Colemans are goin' to be crazy wild. If Pitman can use Rafferty and the Colemans right, he can do

damage. Big damage. Town would never be right again.''
Sam frowned.

"What if the people armed themselves and cleaned out
Rafferty's and then went against Pitman before he was
ready?'' Adam suggested.

"He'd be ready. It's worse'n that. The town is people,
not outlaws. The town couldn't get up on that mesa,
couldn't handle a straight-out war.''

"I believe that.''

"So best maybe it starts and is over. Pitman's move. If he
could be forced into it.''

"You'll get yourself killed, Sam.''

"Could be. It's a chancy way to go about it. I'm not even
sure how it can be done.''

Adam shook his head, frowning. "I want to go
along.''

"Nope. I got my ways. You watch the bank. The town.
Keep it ready if you can.''

"I'm just a tenderfoot, a stranger almost.''

"They know you. Especially now, after today. Oh—
Wagner says you trifled with his daughter's affections.''

"He said what?'' Adam stared.

"Play up to him. Not Missy. Him. Okay?''

"Sam, if I didn't know you I'd say you were a politician,
I swear I would.''

"Watch your mouth, podner. You check with Donkey,
hear me? If the worst happens he'll be in charge.''

Sam rose. Adam leaped up and held out both hands.
"Sam, take care. You've been better than a big brother to
me.''

"Adiós, amigo.'' Sam left quickly, going softly down the
stairs out into the silvery night. There had not been any man
so close to him in many years as he now discovered was
Adam Burr. There was a freshness, an innocence, in the
easterner that Sam had seldom, if ever, noted. It's a learning
thing, he thought with wonder.

He went into the pale night with the moon still playing its tricks with quondam clouds. He went with his conscience clear, because of Renee. He went with sure knowledge that he might not return, and this did not endear him to the task he had set for himself; neither did it deter him.

The faithful, unspectacular dun horse was waiting. He saddled up with great care, examined all four hoofs by light of a dark lantern. There was some jerky in a saddlebag; he knew where there was water. He had half a plan to gain advance knowledge. He rode out of town by the back alleys, staying clear of Rafferty's. He wished he knew one fact: where Jabez Wall was and what was he up to at this hour.

There was evil in Wall; Sam had known it since the transfer of the money at the Long John Mine. Now that Lawyer Deal was gone, Wall was missing an anchor to windward.

Anchor, he thought—a ship. Adam Burr's father's ship. How the mind doth run on. . .

Should he have worked on the unsavory two? Should he have harassed them in order to find truth? He was not a devious man; he lived by confrontations. He had learned a lot about himself through Renee.

Cemetery Jones. He did not love the name or the reputation. He ran back over the shootings—he had never killed a man with a knife or a club. "The short gun is a necessary evil in the West," Renee had said. He lived by the basic laws of survival, and the revolver was his lawyer, his judge. There was Convy. Sam had known that Convy either was sent to kill him or had taken it upon himself to do so. Therefore he had judged him. Knowing he could kill the man, he had not hesitated to do so. He had felt no compunction.

He was riding toward the road leading up to the mesa. Couds came, shadowing the beauty of the moonlight. They were welcome to him. He left the dun beneath the tree he remembered and crept close to the two sentinels, now alert. The news of the debacle at the prizefight had traveled like lightning. He was not surprised; there was certainly a plethora of eager messengers in and around Rafferty's. He edged his way through brush, inch by inch, until he was within earshot of the outlaws.

One grumbled, "My belly ain't use ta the junk we're scoffin'."

"Ain't nobody likin' it. Those goddamn Apaches."

"Rob's got to do somethin' fast."

"Hell's bells, ain't it about time?"

"Frank and Jesse, they're about to have kittens."

"Funny thcy got the same names as the James boys."

"Somebody said they took 'em on purpose. They're kind loco anyways, ain't they?"

"Rob says it's just since Tim got killed. Death of the youngest brother. Somethin' like o' that."

"Rob's smart."

"But we're all hungry. He better do somethin'."

"He'll do it."

They parted to patrol. One came within ten feet of where Sam lay hidden, causing him to draw his revolver. He would have to kill them both if they discovered him. If he did so, the shots would attract those above. It would then be a matter of how many he could dispatch, and which oncs. If he got Rob Pitman they would be without leadership.

If he made his way to the summit and killed Pitman, the entire plan, whatever that may be, would fall apart. He knew that. The remaining Colemans could not hold the gang together, nor did they have Pitman's ability. However, it was a lead-pipe cinch that if he succeeded he would not survive. He cared about survival.

He edged his way like a snake crawling backward. The clouds were now threatening. Out of the mountains a storm could come at any time; it was part of the high plain weather pattern. For tonight's work it would make no great difference, he thought; this was a reconnoiter.

Aboard the dun he rode at a walk toward town. He was uncertain of his next move. He could lie in wait and learn the exact time to strike. He could ride to town and give warning, but if Pitman failed to move it would be a false alarm, and that could be dangerous. He thought of the old fable of the boy who had cried "wolf" too often. He sat for a moment in a clearing at the foot of the rolling hills. It was a mistake.

Indians with rifles, muskets, bows, and arrows rose out of the darkness. They completely surrounded him.

He asked, "Aragon?"

Torches were lit, an ominous ring of flickering light. He peered around, completely surprised. The chieftain appeared, flanked by two warriors.

"Señor Sam."

"I see you took my advice," Sam said, puzzled.

"I did so." Aragon was speaking the language of his people.

In kind, Sam responded. "It was a good thing. The men on the mesa are hungry and desperate."

"They are bad men."

"That's why I told you about the farm. Now you have food and more guns."

"And now we have you to account for the deaths of our young men."

"I see." Sam shrugged. "You want more deaths?"

"We would not kill you without the test."

Sam made a move too fast to be followed and a gun was in each hand. "Okay. Who dies first? After you, that is?"

Aragon raised a hand. "No. The test."

"I am not about to take a test," Sam told him. "You want to die, that's okay by me."

"Then you and many others would die. No. These two

brothers of those killed by you, they would have their chance for revenge,'' the chieftain said.

Sam surveyed the two undersized, wide-shouldered youths. ''Now, that's plumb interestin'. What kind of chance do they want?''

''They will meet you in turn.'' Aragon reached back and someone handed him three long, sharp knives. They were larger than scalping knives but not so heavy as bowies. ''It need not be to the death. First blood will satisfy their honor.''

''That old one.'' Sam remembered it from camp tales when he had spent time with Indians. ''Not truly Apache.''

''Our tribe is not truly,'' said Aragon. ''Ours is a tribe that holds honor sacred.''

''I'll be dogged,'' said Sam. ''Bad as the Christians. Different kinds of religion. Supposin' I refuse?''

''Then there will be blood spilled. I could have you shot down where you stand.''

''You move a muscle and you and plenty others will go down before I die,'' Sam told him lightly, smiling.

''I believe you.''

''This here is called a Mexican standoff,'' Sam said. ''On t'other hand, I got work to do. So lay out your rules.''

Aragon extended a knife. ''The first to draw blood, Señor. That is the rule.''

Sam hefted the blade. It was sufficiently balanced for its purpose. He bent to draw off his boots. The first young Indian stepped forth, naked to the waist, wearing the Apache leggins and red headband. Nobody mentioned his name. The circle closed in to provide better lighting. The clouds now covered the moon as though in disapproval of such mountebanks.

It was not fun to Sam. He was no knife man. The Indian was half his size with twice his skill. Sam poised, awaiting attack. He thought of Renee, of the town, of his own skin.

The Indian was quick. He made a circle. Sam wheeled, maintaining his defensive position. They went around and around until Sam felt himself becoming dizzy.

It was then that the Apache came in low, thumb against the haft, blade pointing up. Sam sidestepped, suddenly throwing a quick left hook.

He caught the surprised Indian on the nose. Blood spurted. Sam stepped back, lowered the knife, bowing to Aragon. "You made the rule," he said.

There was much jabbering, several wolf cries, much jumping around. Aragon hesitated. He looked at the youth, whose nose was rapidly swelling, whose eyes were blurred with tears.

Sam asked, "You want him gutted?"

Aragon shook his head. The bewildered youth retreated, one hand clasping his face.

Aragon said, "It is the rule."

The second opponent stepped forth. He was taller, slimmer than the other. Sam sensed more danger; they had saved their champion for the finale. And people thought Apaches were stupid. After all, they did force the women to do their work while they hunted and fished.

This Indian moved with the grace and agility of a puma. He did not circle; he danced, short steps, right, then left. His footwork was dazzling. He feinted like a professional boxer. Adam would be a better match for him, Sam thought. This was dead serious.

Now the Apache came straight at him. Instinctively Sam threw up his left arm in defense, then immediately knew it to be an error. He jumped to the right and spun around, presenting his own knife hand. The youth ducked and tried to come up inside.

Sam kicked with his stockinged foot. He landed on the Indian's knee and the youth went almost to the ground, recovered, and stepped back beyond Sam's reach.

They measured each other, each now cautious. Sam decided to take the offensive. He swayed, lowered his head, leaped. The Apache was not there.

Again Sam charged. Again he was easily evaded. There were grunts and short cries of exultation from the assemblage.

Suddenly Sam realized that his heart was not in this taradiddle. He did not know his adversary; he had no ill will toward any Apache. It seemed like a bad dream to be standing there bootless, a strange weapon in his hand. When the attack came again he had almost lost concentration. He barely avoided being stabbed in the ribs. He managed to drop a left fist on the Indian's back, throwing him off balance, but was unable to take advantage of the moment.

They sparred; they circled; they attacked and retreated. Time was passing by; there were matters to which Sam knew he had to attend. His patience was running low. His wind was running a bit short. The Indian had more stamina for this kind of work—Sam was a horseman.

Desperate ends, desperate measures, he thought. He stopped moving, stood perfectly still, arms at his sides. He invited attack. The quick Indian responded, coming in with speed and accuracy, the knife held low, ready to stab upward into Sam's immobile body.

Sam stepped to his left. He swung the knife inexpertly but with speed developed in practicing the fast draw. It was an awkward move. The Apache had certainly not expected it, and he floundered.

Sam drove him down with a swinging punch. He put his foot on the youth's wiry body, leaning all his weight. He bent down with the knife poised. A shriek went up from the Apache witnesses.

Sam delicately touched the shoulder of the prone Indian. A drop of blood popped, ran down the brown-red skin. Sam straightened and said cheerfully, ''Reckon that does it.''

For a moment no one moved. Then Aragon stepped forward and held out a hand. Sam put the knife into it.

''Got nothin' against your boy,'' he said. ''He moves real good. Now, is everybody satisfied?''

Aragon said with dignity, ''It is known that you are an honorable man, Señor Sam. You have taken the test.''

Sam donned his boots.

The defeated youth was on one knee, panting, resentful. ''I could have killed you,'' he muttered.

''Not tonight,'' Sam told him. ''Not whilst I'm lookin'. I got serious business ahead.''

Aragon said sternly, ''Señor Sam could have sent you to your reward. He chose not to do so. He will go in peace.''

There was a murmur of assent from the other Indians. Sam buckled on his belt, settling it into place. The torches flickered; several went out. Sam looked around.

''Thanks for takin' the farm. Reckon you'll be gone right soon.''

''We go,'' said Aragon. ''It is good. And you?''

''Trouble in town, or about to be trouble,'' said Sam. ''White man's trouble.''

Aragon nodded. ''The money.''

''Just about it. The money. If you got some, other people want it real bad.''

''It is sad. Go with God,'' said Aragon. ''Your God.''

''You too,'' said Sam. He mounted the dun and turned its head toward the mesa. By now the die should have been cast, he thought. Short rations, unhappy men, Jabez Wall somewhere in the woodpile, another Coleman dead, Rafferty scheming in Sunrise, the town on edge like an old maid at a wedding. He needed to know how far it had gone.

He rode silently in darkness to the path leading upward to the mesa. The sentinels were gone. He needed no further evidence. He headed for town at top speed.

11

They were huddled together in the office of the bank, nestled on Adam's cot. Sally said, "If either Sol or Sam caught us here, we'd be in deep trouble."

"You can't stay long. It's just that I want to tell you."

"Tell me what?" She kissed his ear.

"That I love you."

"You already said that. When I jumped on you after the shots were fired."

"I knew it before then, but you wouldn't talk to me."

"How did you know?" she asked.

"Because."

"Huh!"

"Because you're you. Because you're beautiful. Because lots of things."

"Lots of things are reasons you shouldn't love me."

"Lots of things are past. Your past and mine. Renee knows. Sam knows," he told her.

"Abe Solomon don't know. Missy Wagner and them don't know," she retorted.

"Renee counts. Sam counts. You and I count."

She was silent, taking a deep breath. "I want to be a singer in the East. Where they don't know anything about me. I want to show the world."

He said, "Better show this world. It's a better place."

Again there was a pause. She twisted and clasped her hands between her knees.

He said, "I'm asking you to marry me, Sally McLaine."

"You're what?"

"You heard me."

"Marry you? That's loco."

"Not where I come from."

"Renee and Sam ain't married."

"What's that got to do with us?"

"I . . . dunno." She unclasped her hands. "Adam."

"Yes?"

"Marry *me*? And live here in Sunrise?"

"And raise a family."

"Whooeee!" She leaped to her feet.

He held her about the waist. "I love you and I want to marry you."

She melted into his embrace. She was weeping. She tried to speak, could not. They held tight for long, long moments.

Donkey Donovan walked into Rafferty's and looked hard around. The horse thieves were not in view. Their horses, he'd noted, were not tied to the rack. Rafferty was not behind the bar. The place was jammed, but that was to be expected after the excitement of the day. He departed without taking a drink, amid sullen silence.

He prowled back to the El Sol. Renee was at the piano and there was a celebration taking place. Shaky demanded, "Where's Adam? Everybody wants to shake his hand."

"His hand's sore from wallopin' Grogan," said Donkey.

"Don't seem right without Sam and Adam." Shaky shook his head.

"I agree." Donkey had a beer. Renee nodded to him and he went to the piano. She was playing nothing but lively tunes tonight. However, her ready smile was not in evidence; it was as if her hands wandered without volition.

Donkey said, "Sam'll be all right."

"It seems a long night," she said.

"He knows what he's doing." Two cowboys began squabbling. Donkey went to the bar and stood between them and joshed them back into good humor. Shaky had a Mexican boy helping him and both were running up and down serving drinks.

Shaky said in passing, "Ain't seen the like since New Year's."

"Plenty business for you." Donkey laughed and went back to his rounds.

At the smithy he paused. Holcomb was smoking a corn-cob pipe, leaning on the cannon.

"The boys are havin' a little fun," said the blacksmith. "They won some on Adam."

"Good for them. They work good," Donkey said.

"They better had." Holcomb grinned.

Donkey went on past the bank just in time to see Sally McLaine come out of the alley, walking fast. He overtook her, saying sternly, "You been robbin' the bank?"

She started and said, "Fool. I'm late at the El Sol."

"You sure are. They're roarin' and waitin' to dance."

She said primly, "I ain't dancin' anymore. I'm just singin' from now on."

"Somebody die and leave you a fortune?"

"Better than that." She fled in a gale of laughter.

Donkey walked on. The hotel was dark. On the Wagner porch Missy rocked alone. He called to her and she answered in muffled tones. He roamed the alleys, the back streets. Everyone, it seemed, was either asleep or celebrating. There seemed no in-between.

The El Sol was really jumping. The councilmen were off in a corner. Donkey approached them and reported, "All quiet."

Only Mayor Wagner seemed sober. Frank Nixon said,

"You see that last punch the boy give him? I never seen a better punch."

Tillus said, "That was a punch."

"Best I ever did see," repeated Nixon.

Donkey said to the Mayor, "Sam was worried."

"You seen the Burr boy?" Mayor Wagner asked.

"He's okay."

"Sam wanted him deputized. You agree?"

"Whatever," said Donkey. "Not too many around to do much if anything did happen."

"Nemmine. I wanta buy that Burr boy a drink. A bottle," said Nixon.

Wagner said to Donkey, "Better find him. If he showed himself it might quiet things a bit."

"You sure?"

"Well, after all the yellin' and such."

"Whatever you say, Mayor." Donkey went to the piano. Sally sat close by on a straight chair. A cowboy grabbed at her and Donkey interposed.

Sally said clearly, "I already let it be known I ain't dancin' nor anything but singin'."

Donkey said, "You heard the lady." The cowboy staggered away, shaking his head. Donkey asked, "Where's Adam?"

"Where he belongs, guardin' the bank," said Sally.

"Okay. I got to see him. Mayor wants him."

"Leave him alone," said Sally. "Town's gone crazy."

"He's a hero, like."

"Of course he is. But he's got a job to do."

Renee said, "Sally's right. See him. Let him stay at the bank."

"Sam said to trust him. I guess you're right. That's his trust." Donkey made his way through the happy, celebrating crowd to the street. It was still calm, but there were heavy clouds in the sky. He moved slowly, listening, watching, going to the bank.

Adam was in the office, stretched out on his cot, dreaming of a future life with Sally McLaine. He recognized Donkey and admitted him.

Donkey said, "They're hollerin' for you. Mayor Wagner along with 'em. Sally and Renee got more sense than the men. They said stay here."

"I'm staying. Tell me, how long have you been married?" Adam asked.

"Oh, a long time. Three, four years. Baby's two. I sure do thank you and everybody for helpin' us."

"Is it . . . uh, easy? Being married, having a baby?"

"Easy?" Donkey considered. "Not on my pay." He brightened. "Golly, I plumb forgot. Sam got me a raise. Haven't had a payday yet. It'll be fine when I get the raise."

"I wasn't thinking of money."

"When you got a house and three to feed you'll think on it," Donkey told him. "You goin' to marry Missy Wagner?"

"Hell, no!"

"Course, it's none of my business."

Adam said, "I am going to marry Sally. You're the first to know."

"Sally McLaine?"

"Do you know any other Sally in town?"

Donkey coughed. "It's just I'm surprised. Uh . . . never thought Sally'd marry. Her and her singin' and her talk of bein' on the stage and all."

"She can sing all she wants."

"Yeah," said Donkey. "Well, congratulations. Sally's a mighty fine gal. Knowed her all my life. Knowed her ma and pa before they were killed by the plague."

"Plague?"

"Afore we had Doc Bader. Her folks and mine and others aplenty died of it. Some kinda fever. Our folks were here first, like. Among the first. Dick Land, he helped us kids a lot. It's a good town, Adam. Right now it's crazy-like, with

Pitman and the Colemans and all. But you'll see. It's a nice town.''

''I believe you. I want to live here,'' Adam said.

''That's good. Well, I better be movin' on. With Sam out of it I feel like I'm carryin' too much of a load.''

''I'll be right here.''

''You and me are about the only sober ones in town.''

Donkey waved and went on about his rounds.

Adam, fully dressed, took his position in the office with the vault. He had his rifle, two Colt .45 revolvers, and an empty feeling in his middle. Waiting was the hardest part. He missed the comfort of Sam's presence.

Under the tall tree Jesse Coleman said, ''This here is it. This is where they got Jake.''

Pitman said, ''They were ready.''

''They got Jake. All I want is Jones.''

Pitman said, ''The deputy shot your brother.''

''Jones set it up,'' Frank declaimed. ''Jones sets up everything. That's why they call him 'Cemetery,' damn it.''

''We're goin' in,'' said Jesse.

''Not till I tell you,'' Pitman said.

''Wall, that fool; Rafferty, that slob,'' said Frank. ''You dependin' on them? I say give the word to Shanks and we go in shootin'. The whole town's drunk.''

Sandstorm, Snakehead, Cortez, Absolom, and Montana with his arm in a sling formed around Pitman. None spoke. They sat on their horses with hands on their revolvers.

Pitman said, ''We wait for the signal.'' His voice was quiet but authoritative. ''You want blood; we want money. Jabez Wall is no fool. The plan is laid. We follow it.''

''You trust Wall and Rafferty?'' Frank Coleman asked.

''Now you're talkin' about my own plan. Frank, you already lost two brothers. Are you goin' to listen to me?''

They were silent.

Pitman went on, ''This is takin' a town. It's more'n that.

We have to get away. We have to watch for the double cross. We have to live to enjoy what we get. The Jameses and Youngers couldn't do it. We can if we play our cards right. It's complicated. You understand?''

"We want Jones along with everything else," Frank Coleman said.

"Do you think Jones won't be in the thick of it?"

After a moment Frank nodded. "He'll be there."

"If we don't take him he'll bust it all to pieces. If the townspeople weren't drunk, maybe they'd do it. Jabez Wall was right about that. Now, you do like I told you to do and we'll get away with it." Under his breath Pitman muttered, "Maybe." He knew they could make the attack when the occasion demanded. He knew his own men. He thought he knew how to blow the vault at the bank. He had his own notion about the way in which to escape amid the confusion. Still, the plan was not entirely of his making.

Frank Coleman said, "We'll do what you say."

They sat beneath the tall tree and waited. It was no easier for them than it was for Adam Burr. Pitman looked at his watch.

In the back room of Rafferty's the lamp was smoking and there was no ventilation. Jabez Wall coughed and looked at his gold watch. Big black Izaak adjusted the lamp.

Rafferty was shaking his head. "Why here? S'pposin' this don't work—I'm broke.''

"Dead, more likely," said Wall.

"At least Jones ain't in town. If we can get Rob and his bunch in quick enough . . .''

Wall said, "A few minutes more. It's all timed out. We move, then he moves.''

"He's only got seven men left. Them rustlers, they're no-account in a whizzer like this.''

"There's never been a scheme like this," Wall said. His eyes were shiny, his cheeks flushed. "Timing, it's all in the timing. The right people at the right place. It's perfect, I tell you."

Harp Grogan croaked, "I jest wanta get my hands on that damn tenderfoot one more time."

"You can wrestle his dead body," said Wall coldly. "Don't be a complete damn fool. After this we own Sunrise."

"What's left of it," crabbed Rafferty.

"The good citizens will see there's something left. Then I will take over, after Pitman and his gang are gone."

"If they get put away, you mean," Rafferty said.

"You've got twenty men at least to do that job. The horse thieves may not be much but they know what to do. They know there'll be a payday at Tillus's ranch, stealin' his cattle."

"If Tillus gets killed, you mean."

"He'll be attended to with the rest of the council," said Wall. "Pitman knows what to do about them."

"That timin' you're talking about better be perfect," said Rafferty.

"It will be. It has to be." Wall had to get out of town. He had no intention of showing himself during the fighting. He had to have his share of the loot and get to San Francisco and attempt to confuse the discovery of the evidence left behind by his late partner and lawyer. Wall had a dozen schemes rattling in his feverish mind. His main concern was to get hold of the cash in the bank. Pitman would attend to that, and he would attend to Pitman. One way or another, he had to attend to Pitman. He touched the gun in his pocket to reassure himself that if all else failed he could do the deed himself. It would not be the first time he had shot a man in the back.

He remembered Alexander Burr. It gave him confidence. He had never been a man of action before he had disposed of Burr. That incident had given him the big start he had needed. The pendulum had swung and now perhaps it might again be his time to act. At least Harrison Deal was not there to warn him, to distract him on legal grounds. Jabez Wall was at the end of his tether, and he knew it and was ready to respond. No Cemetery Jones was going to prevent him.

Renee was playing a medley of "Dixie" and "The Battle Hymn of the Republic" in such a manner as to calm the breasts of the two factions that existed in every western town. Sally was sipping a beer and wishing she was with Adam. Shaky and his helper were still rushing drinks. The combination of the worriment about the outlaws and the exhilaration of the victory of Adam over Grogan had truly stirred the town of Sunrise.

Sally said, "I sure wish Sam was here."

"It is getting a bit out of hand," said Renee.

"I coulda made a heap of money tonight."

"You could have got into a lot of trouble, also. All the good folks are in bed, and all the rascals are here. Even the good folks here are out of control."

Donkey Donovan pushed his way through the crowd to join them. "Past closin' time. Shaky's scared to say so. I sure wish Sam was here."

Sally said abruptly, "I'm goin' down to talk to Adam."

She got up and walked past eager, reaching hands, slapping them away. In the street it was rather cool, with the dark clouds hanging ominously low. She started toward the bank. Something caught the corner of her eye. She spun around. There was smoke, then a flicker of fire from Rafferty's Saloon. Men were pouring into the street howling.

"Fire! Fire!"

It was the most frightening word that could come to the ears of small-town people. They were pitifully prepared with one little pump wagon. They had to depend upon a sturdy bucket brigade to control the flames.

As a native Sally knew what would happen. She broke

into a run for the bank, leaving the alarm to others. Adam met her on the street, rifle at the ready.

She said, "Don't move. Those fools at Rafferty's started it. Let the other fools at the El Sol fight it. Watch the damn bank."

"You smell rats."

"I smell outlaws."

He said, "Around back. We're better off back there."

"We're not real good anyplace right now; that I'll bet."

"Inside the bank." They were running. They heard the first shots far down the street. "This is it. They're coming in."

A figure appeared. Adam raised the gun. Abe Solomon said, "No, do not be so quick. The other way."

"But the money . . ." Adam began.

"Money, never mind money. Your skin."

"I have to stay here."

"You work for me. You do as I say."

There was amazing force in the old banker. They turned, however reluctantly, and went to the street again. Sol was with them, gesturing. He walked briskly to his home at the near end of town. He said, "Inside. To the roof with that gun. Like Sam said, the high places, did he not?"

Adam and Sally followed him onto the roof. The fire had already spread to Mayor Wagner's hay, grain, and feed establishment, where it lit up the town.

Sol said, "Wait. Sam will be here. Leave it to Sam."

"There are riders up and down Main Street. There they go, into the bank!" Adam said.

"So. Live flesh is better than all the money in the world."

"I can't stay out of a fight for the town!"

"So when it comes time, when Sam comes, be ready."

The calmness of the old man was soothing. Sally McLaine nestled close to Adam as they oversaw the scene.

There was a crashing of glass as the bank was entered.

People were struggling awake, filling Main Street. Riders with guns cowed them. The fire was raging beyond the town's resources now. They saw Missy Wagner dragging her father away from his establishment; they saw him hit with a bullet and go down, saw her aid him as he crawled to comparative safety.

They saw Donkey Donovan at the door of the marshal's office, kneeling, firing. A horseman went down. Then Sally cried, "They shot Donkey!"

They saw Donkey crab himself inside the door and close it. The outlaws were now cruising the town, shouting for everyone to get indoors if they wanted to live. Two of them rode back and forth; they could hear their voices. "Sam Jones! Show yourself, you sumbitch bastid."

There were no more men coming out of the El Sol. Gunmen at the doors were keeping them at bay. The town was captured, no doubt about it. Rafferty's mob was looting the general store. The fire continued to spread.

"There might be people asleep." Adam saw the bell tower of the church. He aimed and fired rapidly. The bell pealed gloomily into the smoky, overcast night.

Shots came whizzing at the rooftop. The trio flattened themselves as Sally cried, "Where is Sam?"

There was a moment of stunned silence at the sound of church bells. Even the wild riders drew up, as though in awe. From the El Sol came the sound of Renee's piano playing Wagner's "Ride of the Valkyries."

12

It was a desperate time, a fearful time. The affair of the Apaches had delayed him too long. Sam Jones was riding through the woods in the black night that tested his every sensibility. He knew they were ahead of him, and he knew Rob Pitman was far from stupid.

He dared not take the direct road. They would be waiting for him, and he guessed who they would be—who would volunteer, nay insist, that they do the deed. Once before, the Colemans, all four, had ambushed him. He could only hope and pray that the town was not too far lost in celebration to be alert.

Meantime, he could not ride the main road to town. He must prowl through the trees in self-defense. Anger grew in him until he thought he would explode and set the forest afire. He kept the dun to a crawl, stopping now and then to listen.

It was the sound of the bird that brought him to a standstill. He knew the sound. It was not of this region; it was a mockingbird's hoarse trill.

He dismounted with great care. He crept back toward the road, careful of every twig on every bush, every leaf on every clump of chaparral. His eyes were adjusted to the dark; he could make out shapes in the near distance. It seemed an hour before he was certain, but it took less than minutes.

It was their horses he spotted first, one on each side of the road. He waited a long moment, debating. Then he cautiously reached up and felt around until he found a branch of the tree beneath which he had paused. He pulled himself up with utmost care, knowing he would cause a sound sooner or later.

He established himself on the branch. He called loudly, "Jesse! Frank!"

They responded. Their guns blared. Bullets struck the spot he had just vacated. He fired at the flashes of their revolvers.

"God damn you to hell, Sam Jones!" The curse soared to the sky.

Then there was silence. He did not go forward to ascertain the damage done the Coleman brothers. He dropped to the ground and ran to where the dun, as always, waited. Fortunately no wild shot had harmed the animal. He leaped aboard and set out for town.

If the Colemans were dead, which he doubted, that was an end to the feud. That they were out of present commission was the object for now. Haste was required at the moment, and the road to Sunrise seemed miles longer than it could possibly be.

He could smell the smoke before he could see the flames. Now it was his turn to loose every curse he knew upon the heads of those who brought down disaster upon innocent people. He cursed the Long John Mine and himself for selling it to Jabez Wall. He cursed himself for leaving Sunrise on his scouting expedition. And he cursed the poor dun horse for not moving faster toward the town under attack.

Then a calm spread through him, a deadly estimation of what had happened and what might happen. He saw the town and the people in his mind's eye. He tried to estimate what immediate action had been taken, what defense, if any, had been made. Rob Pitman was smart—he would want to make sure of the biggest possible profit; therefore, it was reasonable he would hit the bank at once.

What part Rafferty and his cohorts would take was not apparent to Sam. Somehow he connected it with Jabez Wall. If so, then Wall had put himself somewhere in the middle between Pitman and Rafferty.

If this were true, Wall could either be in clover—or in deeper trouble than he could ever imagine. In any case, he had disguised his operations for the main part well enough that Sam could not put a finger on him.

Now Sam came to the edge of town. Shots were being fired. Men were running; men were riding. He thought of the women, of Renee. He thought of Adam and Sally. He had foreknowledge through Abe Solomon, which gave him a certain satisfaction, but he was more concerned at present with the safety of his people.

With both guns loaded he slowed the dun to a trot and rode briskly down Main Street. He heard cries of recognition. He saw the big black man called Izaak point at him, saw another man aim a weapon. He fired offhand and both went down, the shooter and Izaak. He thought he heard the familiar bellow of Grogan, but could not be sure.

Sam pulled up at the El Sol. He slid down and slapped the dun on the flank, sending it trotting down the alley. He was semiconcealed by an upright post supporting the overhang of the roof of the saloon.

The town was in utter confusion. Amazingly, there was a line of women handing buckets to one another. At their head was Missy Wagner dousing the fire that had already destroyed the main part of her father's business. They were succeeding in keeping the flames from spreading. Riders firing their guns in the street had no stomach for trying to prevent them.

Donkey Donovan croaked from across the street, "Sam! Duck!"

He ducked and a bullet missed his head by inches. Donkey shot a rider from his saddle. From the rooftop of Abe Solomon's house another shot came down to strike a man with a leveled revolver. Sam spun to the door of the El Sol and peered inside.

Two of the outlaws held the customers of the saloon under their guns. One was Montana, one arm in a sling. The other was one of Rafferty's men. Crouching, Sam listened as Renee played some kind of weird march he had never before heard.

Montana said, "That's right, lady. Keep it up. I'll have a time with you later."

"That's Renee," Rafferty's man said. "That's Cemetery Jones's gal."

"That makes it juicier than ever." Montana laughed. "Old Cemetery's molderin' on the trail right this minute."

Each man stood just inside the batwing doors, the better to command a view of the interior. Sam drove in with a shoulder.

One of the doors sent the Rafferty man headlong into Tillus, who kicked the gun from his hand. Nixon scrambled for it and in a split second there was a pileup on the floor. Montana cried out as the other door banged into his injured arm.

Sam raked him with the muzzle of the .44. Blood ran as two customers slugged Montana and snatched away his weapon.

Renee said, "Welcome home, Sam."

"Don't hardly seem homey, all the fuss," said Sam.

Nixon said, "The fire. Everybody out for the fire!"

"The man's right," said Sam. "Best hog-tie these two hombres first. Shaky?"

Shaky put down the shotgun he had grabbed at sight of Sam and said, "Better to shoot 'em instead, but what the hell?"

The Mexican youth produced rope. Men ran to join the

fire fighters, picking up their guns where they had been forced to stack them on the bar.

The shooting in the street now increased to battle volume. Townsmen and horsemen were exchanging fire. Sam took a look and saw the women at work, men joining them. The fire was gaining. Renee came to him.

"Sodom and Gomorrah," she said. "Poor Sunrise."

"You'd be surprised how few people get shot on a dark night with everybody scatterin' around. I got to get to the bank," said Sam.

Sally McLaine and Adam came hurtling through the back door of the El Sol.

"We saw you come in, Sam. The fire—it started at Rafferty's," cried Adam. "But only in front and they put it out quick. After it spread to Wagner's."

"They're in the bank. They're robbin' the bank," said Sally. "They got guards outside. Can we get 'em?"

"Not to fret," said Sam. "Anybody seen Jabez Wall?"

"No sign of him," Adam told him.

"Rafferty? Grogan?"

"No," Sally said.

"Nor the Colemans," added Adam.

"Won't be any Colemans around," Sam told them. "They held me up some, but they won't be here."

Renee asked, "Dead?"

"Or thereabouts."

"You're very calm about it all," said Adam. "What to do now?"

"With all that shootin' it's best we go out the back. You girls stay with Shaky and his shotgun and keep your heads down. All hell's goin' to really break loose in a minute or two," Sam said.

Sally said, "You see Missy Wagner yonder? Her pa got hit early on. I'm gettin' in that line."

Renee said, "Lead on, child."

They were gone like butterflies across the street to the bucket line.

Adam said, "Yes. Well, you can see what they mean."

"Yup."

The women arrived safely, joining the line of bucket wielders. Sam led the way out the rear door. An explosion shattered the ground beneath them.

"That would be the bank," said Sam.

Adam broke into a run. Sam followed more leisurely, his rifle in his hands. There was a tower of smoke coming from the bank building.

"Too much powder," Sam said. "Pitman slipped a bit there."

"We can nail them as they come out."

"Yup." Sam seemed in no great hurry. He led the way up an ally short of the scene of the explosion. They came to Main Street.

Sandstorm, Snakehead, and Pitman ran from the bank. Absolom and Cortez were standing guard on the boardwalk. Pitman yelled, "Head south!"

They all mounted. As they turned south Adam said, "We can't let them escape."

"Should be headin' north to join the Colemans, shouldn't they?" Sam asked.

"But . . ."

The rustlers behind Shanks appeared at the south end of Main Street. Suddenly there was a mob of men led by Harp Grogan blocking Pitman's escape.

"Big war out there." Sam leaned against the wall of the general store.

Adam said, "I'll be damned."

"Some of 'em certainly will," said Sam.

Pitman reversed direction and called, "Charge!"

He had the guns, Sam thought. Grogan ran. Rafferty's men tried to stand, but could not face the steady fire of Pitman's tough crew.

156

Sam said, "Time to move, podner."

He stepped into the open. Adam stood beside him, rifle at the ready.

Sam yelled, "Holcomb!"

The cannon came rolling out from the blacksmith shop. The two boys were at the wheels; Holcomb stood ready to touch it off. Horsemen pulled up, frantic with fear. Men froze in their tracks. Only Pitman was ready to take action. He whirled to fire at Holcomb.

Sam called, "Here, Rob."

Pitman's horse reared. He fought it, brought the gun around to train upon Sam.

Sam fired from the hip. Pitman rose in his stirrups. He clutched at his chest. The horse bolted. Pitman fell sideways, his foot caught in the stirrup.

"That's for Dick Land," said Sam.

The door to the marshal's office opened. Donkey Donovan, an improvised bandage about his shoulder, said, "Got the cells ready anyways, Sam." He was chalk white and wobbly, but there was a wide grin on his face.

"The fire. Everybody attend to the fire," Sam shouted.

The councilmen took charge, rearranging the lines, getting the little pump wagon into use. The general store was looted for any receptacle that would hold water. Sam motioned for Adam to follow him.

"Rafferty?" Adam asked.

"It is somewhat strange. No Rafferty. No Jabez Wall."

"It all happened so quick. Poor old Sunrise."

"Sunrise'll rise again," Sam said.

"It has to." Adam hurried to keep up with Sam.

"People who built it are still here." Sam strode toward Rafferty's Saloon. "You say it started there?"

"Yes. It spread so fast—but it started there."

"We'll have a look-see."

Only the front of Rafferty's had been charred. Sam paused on the threshold, sniffed. "Coal oil."

He ran across the street, then quickly returned. "Even stronger over there."

"You mean it was set on purpose?" Adam asked.

"Sure as hell." Sam led the way back into the saloon. There was very little damage. He said, "Damn fools shoulda burnt the joint to the ground."

"But where are Rafferty and Wall?"

Sam lifted his voice to a shout, "Better get some water in here fast. Rafferty's is goin' to hell in a hack."

There was a moment of silence. Then from the back of the place the door slid open and two figures rushed into view.

Sam said, "False alarm. Just walk up here where you can see what's happenin', gents."

Rafferty and Jabez Wall stood apart, each showing fear that shook them to their boots.

Grogan appeared. He had a gun in his fist. Sam shot him in the arm so that he screamed as he dropped the weapon.

"You were never gettin' much out of this anyway," Sam told the big man. "Triple, quadruple cross was comin'. Didn't you know that?"

Grogan said, "I'll see you in hell, both of you bastids."

"It wasn't my fault," Rafferty said. "The fire started right here."

"We know," Sam said.

"I am not a man of violence," Jabez Wall declared. "I was hiding from all the shooting."

"Sure you were. Waitin' until Pitman robbed the bank. Then you and Rafferty and the rustlers were goin' to take the loot. As if there was a chance of that."

"I don't know what you're talkin' about—I'm a business-man. I own . . . ."

"You don't own anything right now," said Sam.

"I've been here since the fire broke out. Rafferty'll tell you. Ever since . . ." From long force of habit Wall pulled out the gold watch. He flinched. He tried to put it away.

Adam pounced. He seized Wall's wrist and wrested the watch from him. "My father had a watch like this."

"Remember Harrison Deal, what he said to you," said Sam. "Take a good look, podner."

"Father used to dangle this over me when I couldn't sleep," said Adam. "He loved this watch. It was never off his person."

"It . . . it was on the ship," quavered Wall. "I found it. It was on the table . . ."

Sam said, "You ain't much of a liar. A founderin' ship and a watch just layin' there on a table?"

Adam held the watch with its case open. He recited, " 'From Aaron in hopes you understand.' You're my witness, Sam. That's the inscription."

"From Aaron Burr hisself?"

"Father always said he was a much misunderstood man," explained Adam. He snapped open the watch and handed it to Sam, who turned it over into the dim light. "Father was also an adventurer."

Sam said, "Left it behind when he went overboard, did he?"

"The truth!" said Wall.

"You don't know how to spell the word," Sam told him. "But that Harrison Deal, now. San Francisco. And he spoke to Adam. That should shake your crooked bones."

"Lies! All lies!" moaned Wall. "Harrison Deal was a crooked lawyer. No one will believe his lies!"

Sam nodded to Adam. "Put the watch away. It won't be needed, believe me. This jasper will be in jail so long he won't care what time it is." Then he took a step forward and said, "Adam. No."

Adam's rifle was pointed at Wall's chest. "He killed my father, Sam. He had to have done it in order to get the watch."

"He'll rot in jail," Sam said.

"He won't live that long." Adam's finger was tightening on the trigger. He was white with utter rage.

Sam stepped in and roughly knocked the gun away. He pinned Adam against the wall. "No. Not that way."

Rafferty suddenly yanked a pistol from his pocket. Sam threw an elbow, then a fist. Rafferty went down alongside of Harp Grogan.

Sam said, "We could shoot all three of them, couldn't we? Who'd know it wasn't a clean gunfight? Easy pickin's. They'd keep right on callin' me 'Cemetery Jones.' Great Marshal of Sunrise. Fast draw. You like that, Adam?"

Adam's color returned. He cradled the rifle. He shook his head. "You're right again."

"Then let's meander over and make jail room for these three."

They got Grogan and Rafferty to their feet and marched the three men out the door. The people were still throwing water on red flames; black smoke attested that the fire was not under control.

And the storm came.

It's been threatening since I rode out, Sam thought, and now at the last possible moment it's decided to break. It was a mountain storm, coming down in welcome sheets.

People scattered, and now, for the first time that night, laughter was heard in the streets of Sunrise. Renee and Sally rushed through the El Sol and up the stairs to change the wet clothing that clung too revealingly to their bodies. Doc Bader was rebandaging Donkey Donovan when Sam took over the jail.

"Can't accommodate them all," Sam said. "There's that back room at Rafferty's. Nice and comfy. Dark, too."

It took time, but order was restored. A few of Tillus's loyal riders were sworn in as temporary guards, and the council met at its usual table in the saloon and Sam, assisted by Adam, made his report. He had barely begun when Abe Solomon appeared to join the group. He was accompanied by the Holcomb boys who, strong as they were, struggled with heavy suitcases.

Mayor Wagner, wounded but alert, said, "Welcome, Sol. How much cash got blown up?"

"You should ask." Sol motioned to the satchels. "You think I would leave real cash for those nogoodnicks? Right here you got your money, all of it. Adam and me, we took care of it. You see some dirt on it? We buried it. The old-fashioned way for savings."

"You'll need a new building," said Wagner. "I think the town could lend a hand there."

"Building? You don't remember what that building was before we came here?"

"By golly," said the mayor. "It was a whorehouse!"

"And you ran off the girlies and I bought the building. So now we'll start over." Sol beamed upon one and all, accepted a beer, and sat down.

Wagner said, "Damn, this thing hurts. Go on, Sam, tell us."

"Well, I'm goin' to guess a bit. It seems like it was all my fault," Sam began.

"No!"

"Sellin' the Long John to Wall. He sent the Colemans after me and all hell broke loose when it didn't work. Then Rob Pitman needed some help, so he came in for the Colemans. Then Wall and Deal, they went to Rob, who was smart. Not smart enough, but he knew some things. Then I figure Rafferty got into it because . . . well, because he's a crook. An ambitious crook. And he had those jaspers hangin' around and thought they'd be some use. Which they wasn't, in the end."

"You make it sound too simple, Sam," the mayor said.

"The Colemans wanted me. Sure, they were robbers and all, but killin' Tim, y'see, that got their blood up. So they tried, and the last I know about 'em is that they didn't get me and I got some part of them. If I hadn't been held up by those damn Apaches.''

"What Apaches?''

He told them about the test. He ended, "But if they hadn't starved out Pitman, we might still be waitin' for a finish.''

"The Colemans are still alive?'' Mayor Wagner asked.

"Shootin' in the dark, all you know is that if they don't shoot back you ain't in trouble. We can send somebody out to look.'' Sam shrugged. "If it ain't one thing it's another.'' He looked at Abe Solomon. "I'm no businessman nor anything like that, but if Wall did kill Adam's father, wouldn't there be a lawsuit of some kind?''

Sol said, "Truly. Adam may well come into a big bunch of money.''

"Then you two could build a new bank together.'' Sam was beginning to feel expansive now that it was all over. "Seems like that would be a nice endin'.''

Sol said, "It could be.'' He beamed upon Adam. "A smart boy in the bank. Smart buryin' sacks of cash, too, he is.''

Adam said, "I'm happy the way things are.''

Shaky said, "I dunno if you folks know the time, but it's later than that. I say we all get some sleep and take this up again tomorrow.''

"And thank the good Lord we're all here, no?'' said Sol.

"Reckon I'll be sleepin' at the hotel,'' said Wagner, getting painfully to his feet. He nodded toward the satchels of money. "I got enough in there for a new house and a new start.''

"You got neighbors,'' said Nixon heartily. "This here town'll be rebuilt by everybody pitchin' in. Thanks to Sam Jones.''

"One piece of business,'' said Sam. He took the badge from his vest. He fingered it a minute, then said, "Now you're all here, I got a favor to ask.''

"Anything in the world, Sam," the mayor said.

"Tomorrow I want to pin this on Donkey Donovan."

They all voted at once, a resounding "Yea."

When they'd had their last toddy and were gone and the bar was deserted, Sam and Adam looked at each other with raised brows. Shaky also waited, hands propped on the bar.

They came down on cue, first Sally in one of her short-skirted changes of costume, then Renee in a long white coverall of some filmy material. They came to the table but did not sit down.

Sally said, "I'm so tired I could bust all to pieces. I swear I never been this tired since the pigs ate my kid brother."

Adam said, "There's a lot to tell, darling."

"Then tell it to me at the hotel, please."

Adam rose. He took out the gold watch and looked at it. He nodded to Sam and said, "It's time to go, all right."

"Yup."

Adam said, "We're going to be married as soon as possible."

"Sooner," said Sally. "Before I change my mind."

"You won't change your mind," said Renee. "You may be a tiny bit frightened, but you won't change your mind."

Adam and Sally went out, swaying a little, clinging to each other. Sam sat a moment. Shaky raised his brows.

Sam said, "No. I don't think another drink."

"The hotel will be a madhouse," said Renee.

"Yup."

"Everything is finished for now."

"Could be." Sam did not really know about the Colemans.

Shaky showed them his shotgun. "First night in some time I ain't slept with this." He stowed it beneath the bar and went around putting out the oil lamps. "You chillun close up for me? I'm just a tired old man."

"And a good one," Renee said when he was gone into his sleeping chambers at the rear of the building. "A fine man, really. Otherwise, my friend, I wouldn't be here and we'd never have met.''

One hanging lamp at the staircase still shed a small light. Sam asked, ''You believe that? About us?''

After a moment she said, ''Possibly. I don't know, Sam. So many strange quirks to life. Adam and Sally. How odd they two should couple.''

''Shows they both got good taste and good sense.''

''Good sense. Do you think you show good sense doing all those things you do?''

''Good sense ain't got much to do with it.''

''Your way of life. Your involvement. With me it is the piano.''

''You do a lot more'n play the piano,'' he said.

''Not much that means anything.''

''Sally and Adam gettin' married. Maybe that bothers you.''

She shook her head. ''No. That's a good thing.''

''You want to tell me somethin' I don't know?''

''I do. And I don't.''

''It ain't about you and me, is it?'' He felt alarm. ''You don't have to say anything.''

''It's the past.''

''Forget the past.''

''It won't go away.''

''In this country we don't talk about it. You know that.''

The rain pelted down as if to compensate for not coming sooner to assuage the pain of Sunrise. The lamp flickered as she spoke. She said, ''Sam, you must know I don't live off my earnings here.''

''None of my business.''

''I have money invested back east. I also have a name you never heard.''

''I figure you were married back some time.''

''I was. It's—I can't talk about it.''

''You're not married now.''

"True."

He said, "Maybe you want to be married again." It did not sound right coming in that fashion and they both knew it.

"You're sweet, Sam. I love you," Renee said.

Now he could say it clearly. "I love you."

She came close to him. "Imagine you and me married, settling down. Both aware of past matters, dark clouds. It wouldn't work."

"We got money. We could go places."

"Cemetery Jones and Renee the pianist."

"Why not?"

"It is wrong and you know it."

He had no answer. He felt that there was one, but he could not enunciate it. He reached for her.

Frank Coleman croaked from the doorway, "Gotcha. Both of you."

He had a revolver in his hand.

Sam said, "Okay, Frank. But not her."

"You killed my brothers. I'll kill you and yours, you rotten bastid."

"You don't kill women, Frank. It ain't your style." Sam's mind was working at full speed.

"I'm doin' it now." Frank Coleman was braced against the doorjamb, white-faced from loss of blood from the wound Sam had inflicted. "We'll all meet in hell. You done us. I'm doin' you."

Sam shoved Renee with such force that she fell and slid beneath the piano. He dropped to the floor. His gun leaped from its holster. He fired as Coleman fired.

His bullet struck Coleman in the chest and knocked him from his feet. Coleman's shot streaked through the space Sam had vacated.

Sam jumped up and went to the fallen figure. He said, "Frank, you always did talk too much."

Coleman coughed blood. He said faintly, "Damn it all to hell. Cemetery . . . Jones . . ."

He died. Sam turned to see Renee coming toward him, her eyes wide. She fell into his arms, weeping.

He said, "It's all right, dear. No more Colemans."

"There'll always be Colemans," she sobbed. "Don't you see? I can't go through with it, Sam. Now it's plain. Not married. I've been through too much."

"I want to marry you." He wanted it fiercely at this moment. "I need you."

"We need each other. Maybe someday . . . But not now, Sam, darling. Not now."

He took a deep breath. Shaky was in the background, wondering. Sam said to him, "Take care of Frank, will you, please?"

Sam held tight to Renee's hand. "It's all right, dear. It's going to be all right."

He was never more unsure of anything he had ever said. He led her to the stairs and slowly they ascended together. There would be another time; he knew it in his heart. But for now he also knew that she was correct. The rain was still thundering down. Sunrise was saved.

And he was, come what may, still Cemetery Jones.